The Quiet End of Evening

Books by HONOR TRACY

Randon House
New York

THE
Quiet End
OF
Evening

HONOR TRACY

To Dan Binchy

The Quiet End of Evening

One

IT WAS A BEAUTIFUL EVENING IN MAY on Inishnamona, an island off the west Irish coast that has been famous, now and then, throughout the world. Sabina Boxham, aged twenty-eight, was in her garden, in a state of mind bordering on ecstasy. She was handsome rather than pretty, her nose aquiline and her chin strong, but with a fine skin, curly dark hair and soft hazel eyes to make up for it. Her cottage stood hard by the beach shore where the Sound began to widen before flowing into the Atlantic. The little white cabins of the mainland were reflected in the water, wrong side up, the smoke from their chimneys curling downward, their walls trembling now and again as a puff of wind fretted the surface. The gulls were complacently taking their ease, borne slantways along by the inflowing tide; the gray seal lay on her rock in the sun, caressing her pup with a flipper; and the otters slid in and out of the sea or capered about on the shore in their tireless pursuit of enjoyment.

It's wonderful, Sabina was thinking, quite wonderful.

Her happiness was not, however, caused by the quiet lovely scene all around her. Two minutes before, Twomey's lorry had pulled up at her gate and now his men were carrying in her new bath. Last night Mr. Twomey himself had telephoned to say that the tub was there, fresh from Dublin. At first she could hardly believe her ears, for a bare ten months had passed since she placed the order. Colonel Sentence, of Simla Place over the mountain, had waited seven years for a shotgun. By the time Mrs. Rosemary Tooth, of Capri Heights, received her record player she had forgotten why she wanted it. Long before the old Rector's grass-cutter landed, that worthy divine had breathed his last. And yet Miss Boxham's bath—a fancy towny class of a yoke—had appeared, by local standards, with the speed of light! Now she could hardly believe her eyes, but it was there all the same, white, glossy, satin-smooth. She put out a hand and touched it: it was cold, hard, real, a fact in this dreamy place where facts were a curiosity. Really, it seemed too good to be true.

"Will we leave this inside for you then, Miss Boxham?"

But there was no room in the bathroom yet, as Shamus, the plumber, was busy dislodging the old tub. He had been engaged on the work all day, and plaster was heard pouring to the ground as an accompaniment to his tuneless whistle.

"Put it down on the grass for just now," she directed.

"Will you sign for it, please?"

She was about to write her name on the slip when she caught sight of the words "*fittins to foller,*" and a shadow passed over her happy face.

"What's this?" she demanded, frowning. "Where are the taps

and the bung? What good is the bath without them?"

Questions like these lay beyond the scope of Twomey's man. "They mustn't have come from Dublin, I suppose," he said. "You might think of using the old ones."

"Indeed I might not. They're the wrong size altogether."

The warm red face of the plumber appeared at a window and he called for help in lifting the old tub out of the cottage. Twomey's men hurried inside, leaving Sabina to melancholy thoughts of her own.

It had seemed too good to be true; and so, in truth, it was. Before her stretched an era of correspondence and telephone calls. For if Dublin took its time over shotgun, record player, grasscutter, what hope was there, this side of eternity, of getting a couple of taps? To go to Dublin and fetch them would cost nearly as much as the bath itself. The Córas Iompair Eireann bus company had just raised its fares again and the round trip was now equivalent to a package tour of the South of France. The railway station was seventy-two miles off, and although a bus did run there, it was timed to miss the morning train by a quarter of an hour. You knocked around the little county town of Ballycagey until the next train left at four and there was no returning that day, or you hired a car to bring you in earlier, at further ruinous expense. Apart from these considerations, Miss Boxham loathed Dublin with all her heart as being full of people, many of them foreign, and motorcars.

The men were coming out, bearing the rusty old bath shoulder-high, like a coffin. Carefully they set it down on the grass and gaped at it, marveling to think what it must have undergone in the way of usage to get so decrepit.

"Is it the same to you if I go with the lads now, Miss Sabina?" asked Shamus. Like many of the local people, he addressed her in this way because for generations his family had worked for hers. "It's a warm day with the bicycle, and it's near on time for me tea."

"Very well, but will you turn on the water first?"

"Ah, we couldn't do that. You'd be inundated. I've let all the water go out the tank and turned off the pump."

"And how am I to manage until the morning?"

"There's lovely water in the barrel, from last week's rain. And you have the sea."

"Well, you'll please come first thing tomorrow and fix it up."

Shamus was about to give an eager assent when he recalled something which had slipped his mind until then. "Miss Sabina," he said hesitantly. "It's how I can't come tomorrow."

"Nonsense, you must. You can't leave me a day with no bath and no water."

"I wouldn't have wished it," Shamus agreed with a sigh for helpless mankind. "The trouble is only, I'm going to England."

"And you couldn't say so till this!" Miss Boxham screamed.

The grounds for her rage were two. First came the uncertainty as to when, if indeed ever, she was again to enjoy her morning bath. Shamus was rough-and-ready, but thanks to their family association, she could always get hold of him at need. The few other tradesmen on the island would promise faithfully to come, and never turn up. Each took on far more than he could manage, to prevent another from getting it, and all were chronically in arrears. The earliest she could hope for her bath would be one year hence when Shamus returned for his annual holiday; and this depended on his so returning and not, as happened too often now, finding an English girl and settling there for good.

Second was the business of Shamus going to England at all. She would almost rather he went to Belfast—indeed, there would have been sense in that, for he could marry a girl from the south and then, by a yearly offspring, help build up republican force and hasten the doom of Orange oppression. For all that she came of the ascendancy, spoke with an English accent and belonged to the Church of Ireland, Miss Boxham was a fiery nationalist. Her heart was torn by the melting away of Irish manhood all over the west and by the destruction of what she called "the Irish way of life." A year or so back, to her chagrin, the families inhabiting one of the smaller outer islands had been brought across and settled on the mainland. They were tired of being cut off by storms, of the lack of amenity and comfort, of working their flinty fields and climbing the mountain in wind and rain to search for pony or cow; but Sabina mourned the passing of the good old ways and the filling in of the pure old wells. And now this traitor Shamus too was throwing in the towel!

"Why in the name of God did you take out the old one when you wouldn't be there to put in the new?"

"But I thought you were mad for things to be moving, woman dear," the culprit pleaded. "Anyway, Peadar MacGowan is going to sort it for you."

"Is it that one?" Sabina laughed bitterly. "When he's finished with Father Kelly, I suppose."

A decade had passed since Father Kelly entrusted Peadar MacGowan with the rebuilding of a burned stack, cause of such volumes of smoke that by now the poor man was all but kippered; and where Father Kelly failed, who might hope to succeed? But it appeared that Peadar would come at once to Miss Boxham, in consideration of a small favor that Shamus had done him.

"At once?" queried Sabina, familiar with the local turns of speech. "He'll be up to me in the morning, then?"

"Well, now—he has the turf to cut."

Three times in the summer the repose of the region was shattered by bursts of activity. With the first dry weather the people went to the bog to cut and spread their turf for the winter's fuel; later, when it was hard, they must drag it to the roadway for lorries to collect and leave at the villages; and later still, as the weather allowed, they had to cut, shake and store the hay.

"That will be three weeks, anyhow," Sabina moaned, for the handful of men remaining helped the families of those who had gone. Three weeks of filling her pots from the barrel, dragging them through the house, heating them on the stove, washing herself in a basin, letting the household things pile up! And suppose the weather held and the barrel ran dry, then she must lower a bucket into the well itself, whose surface twitched and trembled with nasty life, and boil each unfiltered drop before she drank it, as well as kill herself hauling it up. Her mind raced on to where the well itself gave out, which happened as often as the island enjoyed anything like a summer. Happily, this was rare, about once in eight or nine years, but it always began in May with a long fine spell like the present. No doubt by the time her bath was installed there would be no water to use. She would have to buy it by the drum at extortionate rates from pirates at the farther end of the island, the tourist end, where the council had put in a main supply. Her poorer neighbors would climb the mountain, looking for the last thin trickle of a stream, while their cows bellowed for thirst and their dogs lay panting in the shade.

Twomey's men had loaded Shamus' bicycle onto the lorry and were anxious to be gone.

"I wonder you'd bother with a place like England," was Sabina's parting shot. "I'm sure Irish life is good enough for me."

"Arrah, ma'am. You can't fill a pay packet with Irish life." He was safe on the lorry before he delivered a parting shot of his own. "I wouldn't use the light in the bathroom, Miss Sabina. There's a small little stretch of the wiring exposed."

This proved to be an understatement. A whole side of one wall had been ripped away and the wires hung down in a loop, their protective covering gravely damaged. It was hard to conceive why Shamus, who had merely to disconnect the taps and pry the bath legs from their concrete bases, should have set about the wall in the first instance. All his work had this touch of idiosyncrasy. The last of the water in the cylinder dropped eagerly onto the floor, forming a muddy pool. Bereft of their home, earwigs and spiders ran furiously to and fro.

To ease her mind, Miss Boxham went to ring up Milo Twomey. That gentleman owned the single large emporium on the island, and he was rung up so often, on such a multitudinous range of subjects, that he had evolved defenses not easily broken through.

"Miss Boxham! Wasn't I thinking of you this minute!" he cried. "The first small salmon of the year are after coming in."

The news merely fanned Miss Boxham's indignation. She was extremely fond of salmon and had been at Mr. Twomey for some time past to let her know as soon as the small ones started running; and well she knew that but for her telephone call this afternoon, he would never have breathed a word.

"My bath has arrived, but not the fittings," she said frostily. "It's of no use to me at all."

"No fittings, that's bad. I must look into this," Twomey said. "I'll have a word with Dublin and ring you back."

"Were the fittings ever ordered?"

"I'd say they were, at a guess," Mr. Twomey assured her. "The lad that put the order in is gone to England. But what d'you think of the bath itself, Miss Boxham? Isn't it a masterpiece? You'd find no better in Buckingham Palace."

"I don't want to be waiting another whole year."

"Ah, you won't, you won't," the soft voice purred. "But what's a year, all the same?" Where time was concerned, the Twomey perspectives were not unlike those of the Vatican. "It's past and gone in a flash, just like ourselves. Did you hear that Joe Gallagher died, poor man? Ah, he'd no good to do and he's better off where he is, please God."

Miss Boxham was not to be thrown off course so lightly. "Perhaps your lorry could pick up the taps when next it goes to Dublin?"

Milo could just about see himself sending a lorry to the end of the world for a pair of old taps. "The very thing!" he gladly assented. "We'll do that for you, Miss Boxham, with pleasure."

"And when will it go?"

"I couldn't tell you offhand, but I'm sure it won't be long." Here Mr. Twomey selected another fly and cast again. "And you're not at the meeting, then? I'd have gone to it, all right, only I'm tied to me desk."

This time the trout rose at once: it all but leapt from the water.

"The meeting!" Miss Boxham cried in anguish. What with the surprise delivery of the bathtub and the consequent dialogue with Shamus, the meeting had quite gone out of her head. Never before had the Action Committee assembled without herself being there, and the deliberations today were of particular and far-reaching importance. "Do your best for me with the taps, then," she concluded in haste. "And send up a three-pound salmon."

With that she hurried out to the meadow, to catch the pony and harness him to the trap. One of her reasons for employing this type of conveyance was that she really preferred it to any other. For a time after the war while gasoline was scarce, her father had kept one, and some of her earliest childhood memories were of happily jogging around with him. But another, stronger reason was that it was comfortless and inconvenient, like the furnishing of the cottage itself, and therefore true to the Gaelic tradition. The spirit of that tradition, however, burned bright in Finn, the pony, too. Peacefully he munched at his grass until she was within a few yards and then, with a derisive neigh, cantered off to the end of the field. His chronic oppositionism was never so marked as when she was pressed for time. Argument and appeal were in vain, and, fuming, she returned to the shed for oats and apples. Even with this inducement, the cob was thinking it over a full half-hour before he gave in. It was long after six when at last he was between the shafts of the trap and Miss Boxham was urging him up the dusty road over the hill to Pio Moriarty's Up-To-Date Lounge, where the meeting was scheduled to start at five.

Two

INISHNAMONA, or the Isle of Turf, is about two-thirds the size of Achill, and as any of its children will confirm, at least four times as beautiful. Yet it is not to be found on the map. The bog, mountain, lake, streams and hamlets comprising it certainly figure, but as part of the mainland, because up to about eight months before this story opens, that is what they were. Then the island was a peninsula, of bizarre if not unique formation, the neck being a narrow strip of limestone some eighty yards long, twelve yards wide and level enough to serve as a road.

The change of status was due to no geological convulsion, earthquake or other natural cause. In common with all the west, the region was slowly dying. The fish had moved away, the stone quarries were shut, the tiny farms no longer produced a living, and there was no industry apart from the collection of wrack, the seaweed being treated elsewhere. This state of things was no one's fault. It was the lot of primitive communities in the world of today. But there was a little band of local patriots who would not accept that and preferred to blame the Government, which by now had superseded England as the object for their rancor. In protest, then, against Dublin's cruel indifference, they had, with generous outside help, blown up their rocky causeway and declared themselves an island.

Their first aim in this, which was to get themselves talked about, was fully achieved. The exploit made front-page news at home and abroad, and they fairly reveled in their sudden dramatic prominence. Delightful as it was, however, it was also brief. After a very few days the press forgot them and they soon found out that far from solving their problems, they had merely created a fresh and extremely grave one.

The beauty of their land, with its magnificent cliffs and curious rocks, its banks of fragrant gorse or wild rhododendron, the hedges of scarlet fuchsia, the mountains purple with heather, and the dazzling blue sea, had formerly attracted tourists from England, Europe and America. From Easter onward the roads were crawling with cars on their way from one beauty spot to the next. In taking their spirited action, the patriots had insufficiently pondered the effect on this, their only source of income apart from seaweed, the dole, or remittances from England. At low tide the island could still be reached on foot by those willing to remove their shoes and stockings and risk a fall on the slippery jagged rocks, but those coming by car must wait for the ferry, a weary, wheezing affair that inched its way over the Sound as if it hardly thought to arrive, and whose skipper was frequently absent on his other duties of rate collecting.

Consequently, the stream of summer traffic had died away

to a mere trickle, and to remedy this, as well as the whole flight from the region, the Action Committee was formed. As was natural, the members were not moved purely, or even mainly, by idealistic concern. They were hoteliers and shopkeepers whose trade was dwindling, schoolmasters who foresaw that their schools would be shut, small contractors who did not know where to turn for their labor. Apart from Miss Boxham, the few local gentry took no interest, their experience leaving them doubtful of schemes which might call for application, sobriety and public spirit. As for the local people themselves, their attitude was one of ribaldry. The young crofters thirsted to get away, men of working age had mostly gone, and the old were content to live out their days on the English pension.

It was to discuss the dearth of visitors that the Committee was meeting now. They were getting into June, with a mere handful of strangers around, hitch-hikers and other riffraff, and bookings ahead but a fraction of what they should be.

"I don't understand it at all," Pio Moriarty, the Chairman, remarked, despondently shaking his head. "Is it the prices charged? Sure, everyone knows he'll be stung on a holiday, and you have to get what you can while you can, with the long old winter before you."

As a matter of principle, it was never so much as hinted that the blowing up of the causeway bore on the case. To do that would have been to suggest that the glorious action itself had been a mistake, and the official line, adhered to by all the right-thinking, was that in the circumstances created by Dublin, nothing else could have been done. There would, further, have been the risk of offending Pio Moriarty, who, as everyone knew, had taken part in the operation. As everyone knew, yet did not know, for Pio himself was of two minds about it. At the inquiry he had sworn, along with numerous witnesses, to having spent the whole night in question waking a cousin upcountry. He had never heard even one of the four mighty explosions which made the welkin ring and brought everyone out of bed in the belief that the world was ending and the devil collecting his own. But when the inquiry was closed, and the guards and the soldiers stopped prowling and prying, Pio let it fall, cautiously, bit by bit, that his had been the brains behind the plot, his the gallant thumb on the detonators. This second version in no way canceled the first, to which Pio had recourse whenever expedient, nor did anyone venture to choose between them but accepted both as equally valid and true.

In probing the emergency, then, they ignored the severance of links with the outer world. They put the blame on American politics, English caprice, Continental allurements, the Orange Peril, Bord Failte and Dublin, and on the climate, which they were half inclined to believe was Dublin's doing as well. But this afternoon, when they had trotted over the familiar course yet again, the teacher Niall McCarthy had something to say. He was from a mainland village seventeen miles away and spoke with an alien's detachment. "All very fine," he observed, "but what you're after saying applies as much to Achill, and Achill is having a bumper year."

There was a pause while the Committee digested this. "Achill *says* it's having a bumper year," the Chairman then corrected Niall, as if deploring his simplicity.

"I'd say so, too," Niall rejoined, unshaken. "I was over there

Sunday, and the beaches were crawling. Crawling!"

The Committee members then bethought dismally of their own four beaches, mile upon mile of gold or silver sand, hard and pure and untrodden, with nothing to see but tumbling waves and birds flying overhead.

"I'd say that was an exception," the Chairman argued.

"It was on the paper how Alcoholics Anonymous held a monster rally near Westport Saturday. They'll have gone on to Achill after, and made a job of it."

"Let them hold the next rally here, then," said Niall. "There's candidates enough."

But the Chairman was quick to pounce on the flaw in that notion. "Maybe there is, but anonymous?" He reeled off a list of names. "What's anonymous about all that, will you tell me?"

Here the door between the lounge and the public bar opened a little and the tip of a scarlet nose appeared. "When you're ready," a hoarse voice said.

"Have patience, man, we're in committee just now."

"I heard me name a moment since," the voice went on, "and I didn't like what was tied to it."

"Our proceedings are confidential," said the Chairman.

"And privileged," said Jerry Maguire, an attorney.

"The divil fly off with your privileges and proceedings," growled the voice. "The drinking hours are from . . . from when you open till when you shut. That's the law of the land, and I'm entitled to get me stout, for all your Committee."

"And I'm entitled to refuse a man that's had enough," the Chairman pointed out.

"Sure, that's what nobody ever had yet," riposted the voice. "When you're ready!"

The Christian Brother leaned forward and whispered urgently in Pio's ear, "Arrah, draw his pint and stop his gob, or we'll be here all evening."

Sulkily Pio compiled. Every time the Committee met, its work was disrupted and its dignity marred by his having to quit the chair and draw pints for the all-day soakers, who then put fantastically garbled tales around as to what it discussed and decided, bringing it into contumely and causing endless mirth. But the bar was not allowed to close and none but he could mind it; producing and rearing eleven children had so addled his wife's poor brain that she could neither recollect prices nor give back change, and since he clung to the sweets of office, he had to accept the drawbacks with such grace as he could.

Having drawn the pint for the man in the public bar and adjured him to make it last, he returned to his civic duties to find that Rowty Mulligan, the vet, had blossomed out into brilliance. "We'll have to offer them more than scenery," he was declaring. "Romantic scenery—the whole of the west is polluted with that. We must offer them something unique, something they'll get nowhere else in Ireland, or the rest of the world either."

"There's a lot in that," Pio agreed, resuming the chair. "Only, what'll it be?"

"Well now, look-at. There's some German place, how's this you call it, where they have a Passion play. Booked clean out for years ahead, standing room only. We'll have to get something to match it."

"We'd best keep religion out," Niall McCarthy objected. "There's no end of snags in religion."

"And did I say anything about religion? I only gave the Passion play as an instance. Of course we'd want something Irish."

There was a murmur of general approval, and all began eagerly making suggestions. Someone proposed a survey of Irish history, to include such items as the trial of Robert Emmet, the eviction of starving peasants in Connaught, the torture of a saintly hedge priest and the martyrdom of the leaders of 1916, but this was crushed by the Chairman, who observed that the English formed the cream of the trade, and to depict them as a bunch of ravening monsters was a queer old way of making them feel at home.

"Wait now!" cried Rowty Mulligan. "A pageant of the life of St. Patrick! Here in the west, cradle of his finest exploits! We'll be killing two birds with one stone—he's both our national saint and a local celebrity."

The notion was well received by all except Niall McCarthy. "There isn't a terrible lot that's really known about St. Patrick," he demurred. "Any book you'd read, it's saying how the other books are lies."

"Don't mind them," Rowty replied. "We know the essential facts, how he banished the snakes and cursed the fish and threw the demon off the mountain. All good colorful stuff, and vouched for."

"Where will we put it on?" inquired the Christian Brother. "You'll need space for that kind of work. It wouldn't address itself to the parish hall."

"Why couldn't we make an open-air theater out there, on the side of a hill?" asked Tomo O'Shea, the contractor. He had a bulldozer and other costly equipment rusting away in idleness.

"We could flatten out the stage in a hollow and then construct row upon row of seats all above it."

"And the audience catching their deaths," remarked Niall. But he had lost the ear of the meeting.

"I'll be composing the words," Rowty volunteered, flown with a sense of achievement. "Now I have the cattle tested, there's time on me hands."

Everyone started talking at once, making suggestions and offering help, until Pio called the assembly to order with a brisk rap of a bottle on the bar.

"Before we do anything else, we'll apply for a grant to Bord Failte," he said, amid fervent applause. "Rowty can be writing away if he wishes, but we'll leave the technicalities until we know what's coming in." With that he declared the meeting adjourned and asked the gentlemen what it should be, and they were happily buying each other drinks when at last Miss Boxham drove up in the trap.

Her fellow members were somewhat puzzled by her. They thought it well to have one woman with them and were not ill pleased that she was a Protestant and a lady, handsome, young, with a bit of money and own sister to your man in the Big House. But those very attributes which did them credit stood in the way of their making her out. It foxed them why she should trouble herself and what she could possibly hope to gain. She was not looking for contracts or rake-offs, and if every local business shut and every local man went abroad it would hardly affect her at all. You'd think she'd be looking around for a husband and getting her life into shape, but she was never seen with a fellow. There was something behind it, they assumed, but they couldn't fathom what. Nor was it just her being there that baffled them; they were equally at a loss to grasp her point of view. She was apt to be what they described as "airy-fairy," and yet she would be suddenly, brutally, down to earth at times when they themselves were soaring in flights of imagination.

Of this second characteristic she proceeded to give an example now. Rowty's scheme on the whole met with her approbation. It offered a chance of talking down to the tourists, and this softened a little the humiliation of needing them so much. But when she heard of Rowty's appointment as official bard, up she got, ready with buckets of water at once.

"Has Mr. Mulligan done any writing before?" she inquired, disagreeably blunt as usual.

Mr. Mulligan confessed that he never had.

"Arrah, what harm?" protested Pio. "He'll do it as well as the next. It's not like a trade you'd have to learn."

"If that were so, half Ireland would be authors," replied Miss Boxham. "I mean no disrespect to Rowty Mulligan, but it might be as well to commission a script from somebody of experience."

"There's no such man in the country," Pio pointed out.

"Then we must look for one outside."

"And that's half the grant down the drain before we get it!" Pio objected. "I'm not supposing Rowty's a Shakespeare, but he'll knock something out for us, and just for the glory alone, amn't I right, Rowty boy?"

The bard signified his readiness to work for glory alone. "Sure, what's an evening lost when times are quiet?" he asked amiably.

Miss Boxham allowed the matter to drop and went on to

something else. "You spoke of a grant," she said. "What grant was that?"

Pio informed her of the Committee's decision regarding this, only to receive a further slap of cold water.

"Why do you imagine we'd ever get one?" Miss Boxham demanded. "It's not as if we were building a fancy motel."

"Ah, there'll be a grant!" "There must be a grant!" "There's always a grant!" came from her fellow members in startled chorus.

"We're doing this for the good of the country," the Chairman said, to murmurs of approval, "and it's only right if the country supports us."

Now, in the disconcerting way she had, Miss Boxham switched to the airy-fairy. "I disagree altogether," she declared with vehemence. "The country cannot afford these eternal grants. It's coming to this, that no one in Ireland will lift a finger unless the Government bribes him. We are becoming a nation of subsidized loafers—we, that were saints and scholars when the English were running about in woad!"

She's away, thought Pio. "You're right, Miss Boxham, of course, and we're all of us with you," he said, smiling uneasily.

"Everyone connected with the pageant should give his services free, and we should meet any expenses ourselves," she continued. "Then it will be our own and we can all take a pride in it, without going cap in hand to a soul."

"That's a fine, elevated point of view you have there, Miss Boxham," Pio applauded, trying to conceal his dismay. "If we only get the people to see it!"

"They will, if we set the example," Miss Boxham affirmed.

"When they see us making sacrifices, they'll want to make them too."

For a moment the members were speechless, but in the next they warmly expressed their agreement, pledged themselves to act in conformity and remarked on their great good luck in having her there to guide them. They well knew that in certain respects she had no more sense than a child, but they also knew that things would be done as they, and not she, decided.

As long as a lady was there, the soakers in the public bar had respectfully held their peace. Now, as she took her leave, the clamor for drink was resumed, noisy and urgent as the croaking of frogs after a period of drought. Hoarse voices appealed for haste or demanded priority, as might the wounded left on a field of battle. Listening to them, and Moriarty's calm, waggish rejoinders, she had a disagreeable sense of futility, as if the Committee discussions had been merely a game, interrupting the true business and purpose of life, but now, mercifully, over. She was glad to exchange the sour fumes and dull light of the place for the smell of pony and harness leather in the warmth of the summer evening.

Moriarty's Up-To-Date Lounge stood at the crossing of two roads, one a rough stony track leading from Sabina's village to another, similarly down-at-heel, on the farther shore, the second a well-surfaced highway on the main tourist run. It was the latter, woefully free of traffic these days, that she must take to reach her brother's house. Bowling along, she mused upon the recent discussion and the different viewpoints that had emerged. These were not simply in the practical question of the grant but in the very nature of the project itself. For her, it was a chance to affirm Ireland's spiritual hegemony, her civilizing missionary role through the centuries, never more needed than in the howling pagan world of today. The stranger should feel her greatness, past and present; he must learn to know her as she was, not as she appeared to his dull and materialist eyes. There was a deplorable tendency to see her in terms of incompetence, laziness, avarice, deceit and charm, but these were purely external. The screen must be drawn aside, affording a glimpse of the naked Irish soul in all its grandeur. So Miss Boxham thought, but the Committee talked like footballers, on fire to prove themselves better and faster then the visiting team. Not one had been to Oberammergau or even knew its name, only Mulligan had heard of the Passion play; yet now, to a man, they dreamed of wiping Oberammergau's eye. She would have her work cut out to wean them from this childish frivolity to a due sense of their cultural mission, and she was still thinking the problem over when the cob turned in at the iron gates, hospitably open, of Mount Skellin, her childhood home.

Three

FROM THOSE GATES, a long green tunnel of densely growing shrubs led to the gardens and the house. It also connected, or separated, two worlds as different from each other as well could be. Sabina had been conscious of this from early childhood on, but in her younger days it was a simple matter of Them and Us. As she grew up, however, she saw that the world of Us, apparently the more real and more solid, in fact was in ruins. The inhabitants were taking refuge in flight, withdrawal or make-believe, none of which suited her lively and positive nature. Deliberately, she crossed over to the world of Them, or tried to do so, with the result that by now she was nowhere at home. She felt as much but would never, even to herself, admit it.

No sooner did the trap debouch into sunlight at the farther end of the tunnel than she saw something vexatious. Her brother, Thomas, stood on the parapet which surrounded the rose garden, flying a kite. It was a thorn in her flesh, his idling the days away in trivial amusements, when he ought to be throwing himself heart and soul into local affairs. Five years before, he had come down from Oxford with a splendid degree and his tutor's augury for a yet more splendid future, but in that same year their father suddenly died and Thomas inherited. With his brains and his position he should have been first in the neighborhood, but he chose to be nothing at all. Worse, he was wholly indifferent to the griefs of his native land and the iniquities practiced against it by others. If she spoke of emigration or partition, he smiled or yawned; he affected to believe that Fianna Fail, one of the two major parties, was the name of a jig; and of Ireland's spiritual heritage he apparently had never heard.

The case was aggravated by the fact that she was a year older than he, that only the accident of sex prevented her from standing where he stood and exercising all those functions he neglected. Nor, in her view, was there any good reason why the usual order should not in this instance have been waived. The house was not entailed, nor was it supported by lands that might require a man's attention. The original building was put up by an ancestor who had done well in Nelson's navy: the turrets and battlements which gave it a post-Baronial look were added by another, who had done still better in the Indian administration. The upkeep had always been met by accumulated funds of one kind and another, and thus the place could hardly be thought of as an ancestral home or family seat: so she argued. But her father, and still more her mother, thought differently, and at Paul Boxham's death everything passed to Thomas except an income for life to herself.

Her brother turned his head at the clatter of hooves and

waved his free hand. "What do you say to this?" he called out. "I made it myself!"

Sabina halted Finn and surveyed the kite with disparagement. "I should have thought, with so much time to spare, you could have mown the grass," she observed. The terraced lawns, which fell away to the trout stream on one side and to the shore on the other, were sadly neglected.

"The grasscutter is broken," replied Thomas at once, as if this fact alone had prevented him from doing that very thing. "Shamus will have to mend it."

"Shamus is going to England tomorrow," Sabina informed him, in a tone that seemed to hold him responsible.

"Then he must mend it tonight, mustn't he?"

Sabina jumped down from the cart and advanced toward her brother with the light of battle in her eye. "Is that all you have to say, when he's worked for us all our lives?"

Resignedly, Thomas began to haul in his kite. "Come off it, Sabby," he begged her. "What d'you expect me to say? 'Tis a shockin' thing altogether how the flower of Irish manhood does be ebbin' away to that pagan counthry beyant'? I'll leave that to Moriarty and your other bowsie friends."

"Of course you make a joke of everything that doesn't directly concern yourself." It galled her that Thomas could put on a more convincing brogue than she. "I realize that the loss of our men is of no importance, or the probable death of the island either. But haven't you a thought to spare for Shamus, having to leave his home and kin and work in that ghastly England?" Here, however, she broke off, checked in her gallop: her own first thought, she recollected, had been for her bath, not for the sorrows of Shamus.

Thomas lazily turned his head and addressed an unseen presence on the other side of the parapet. "Did you hear her, Harry? Are you not going to stick up for your native land?"

A figure rose from a deck chair placed among the bushes and bowed politely to Sabina across the wall.

"This is my friend Harry Buckle, who has come to stay," said Thomas. "And this is my sister, Harry. She's fonder of me than you might suppose."

"I couldn't see him down there, could I?" Sabina defended herself tartly. "I'm sorry for what I said, Mr. Buckle."

"It's for me to be sorry that you have cause to say it, Miss Boxham," said Mr. Buckle, bowing again. He had a precise way of talking that went with his whole appearance: the round and rosy, somewhat eighteenth-century face, the blond silky hair brushed loosely back in the Shelley manner, and the clear blue eyes that gazed out on the world with childlike candor. His clothes were restrained, by contemporary standards, and even elegant, but to Sabina they looked like fancy dress. She took an instant dislike to the wearer.

"Which parts of England do you know best?" he went on placidly.

To her annoyance, Miss Boxham felt her face growing pink. "I've never been near the place at all," she replied, with a toss of the head.

"Which never prevents an Irish person from knowing all about it," smiled Thomas.

"And haven't we cause to know?" she flashed at him.

" 'We'?" Thomas rolled an eye over the ample contours of Mount Skellin.

"Let us not speak of my disagreeable country," the urbane Mr. Buckle proposed. "I am so greatly enjoying yours."

Thomas descended from the parapet with the captive kite on his arm and gave Sabina a languid kiss. "I insist on your staying to dinner," he said in a voice that had no insistence about it. "We have a little treat for you." Twomey's needed no urging, in Mr. Boxham's case, to send up the pick of the salmon. "At least I hope we have—there's a new cook. Take that animal out of the traces and put him in the stable while I see about something to drink. We were out at tea time; poor Harry must be parched."

Sabina demurred. "I wanted to talk to you privately," she said in a resentful tone, as if Mr. Buckle should have foreseen as much and refused her brother's invitation.

"And so you shall. But don't try and involve me in anything, there's a good woman. All attempts of that kind are doomed to failure."

He was really hopeless, Sabina thought, leading Finn through the haggard to the all-but-derelict stables. Evidences of decay were to be noted on every side. Sagging gates, broken fences, mossy roofs, the shrubbery choking for want of pruning knife and ax, the orchard yielded up to rust, curl and lichen. It was true that labor was not to be found, but there was much that one man could do for himself if his heart were in it. In her brother's shoes, she would have struggled on till she dropped. But there he was, flying kites like a boy of fourteen, with the place all round him screaming for help!

She ought to have stayed on when her father died, as Thomas

had suggested, and would have done so, too, had she known what the future held. The stumbling block had been her mother, inert and feckless as Thomas himself, for whom she had never cared. Julia Boxham was but fifty and of an iron constitution, so presumably would cast her shadow for many long years to come. But like her son, she could spring to action in the rare event of her deeming it to be called for. A year after her husband died, her golden Labrador became entangled in the water lilies on the lake while out for an evening swim; Mrs. Boxham plunged in to the rescue and lost her life. By then Sabina had bought her cottage and was up to her ears in building and improving. Even so, she would happily have consented to return, but Thomas was too lazy and she was too proud to bring up the matter, and things had continued as before.

She tied the pony, rubbed him down and went back to the front of the house, where her brother and this guy of an Englishman were enjoying drinks on the lawn. Mr. Buckle rose to his feet.

"Where are you going?" asked Sabina, who had forgotten polite usage.

"Nowhere—he has some good manners, that's all," her brother replied. "I wish I could say as much for myself. What would you like?"

Made to feel silly again, Sabina took Mr. Buckle in deeper aversion. "We poor savages aren't used to society ways, I'm afraid," she informed him. "Do please sit down. I won't drink, Thomas, thank you. I shall do some jobs in the garden until it is time for dinner."

"Excellent idea!" her brother applauded, leaning back in his chair and closing his eyes.

"Are you in need of any assistance?" Mr. Buckle inquired.

"Not of the unskilled sort," was the damping reply; and Miss Boxham retired in search of gardening tools.

Mr. Buckle resumed his seat with a pensive air. "I cannot feel," he remarked, "that I am altogether a smash hit with Miss Boxham."

"Poor thing, you must excuse her," Thomas said, laughing. "She hates England, without having been there. She hates all Englishmen, and I doubt if she's met a dozen. But Irish nationalism is catching, like measles. Her head is crammed with nonsense and she keeps some very strange company. Still, what is she to do with herself? There's no one here for her to marry, and she won't go away." Having thus comfortably disposed of Miss Boxham's dreams and aspirations, he opened an eye and said with unwonted gravity, "But not a word to her of what we were discussing. Truly, I think she'd go out of her mind."

Mr. Buckle promised to do nothing that might lead to such a disaster, and the two young men drank and chatted agreeably until it was time to get ready for dinner.

Formal meals at Mount Skellin, inasmuch as they could be so described, were announced indoors by means of an Indian gong, lifted a hundred years ago from a Hindu temple, while those outside were summoned by the tuneful notes of a hunting horn, blown from the top of the front-door steps. These instruments were played by Maggie and Bridie, respectively, middle-aged twins employed in the household whom no one at any other time could tell apart, for the fact that Bridie could use the horn and Maggie could not was apparently all that distinguished them.

Now the coo of the horn came to Sabina's ears as she pulled and slashed at the docks and thistles in the shrubbery; thankfully dropping her hook, she made for the pump, rinsed her hands, smoothed her hair and, her toilet complete, joined the men in the drawing room.

Once in it, she was conscious, as so often, of a peculiar ambivalence of feeling that was beyond her power to analyze or overcome. On finding that Thomas and Mr. Buckle had changed into evening clothes, she automatically sniffed, and at the same time it pleased her that they had done so. She would have said, and believed, that the scale and luster of Mount Skellin, with the family portraits and family silver, the Chippendale, the Sheraton and all such trappings of wealth long and tenaciously held, were as nothing to her; and yet, in a mysterious way, their presence buoyed her up. Had anyone suggested that Mr. Buckle's opinion could matter a ha'penny, she would have laughed outright; nevertheless, there was a certain gratification in displaying to him the Boxham grandeur, so different from the middle-class hugger-mugger in which, doubtless, he lived himself.

It was, accordingly, with a somewhat regal air that she led the way to the dining room, noted for a splendid view from the wide bay window. Here was an oak refectory table, which could accommodate thirty people with ease, and on it a silver candelabra of rare beauty, though black for want of polish; two antique chafiing dishes, similarly in need of attention, stood on the massive sideboard; and on the mantelpiece was a superb Empire clock, which permanently said a quarter to five. A gaunt woman in a checked apron stood with folded arms behind the master's chair, impassive like a Nubian sentry.

"I wonder why there are cups and saucers," said Thomas, surveying the spread with interest. "I looked out the wine and left it in the pantry. And, dear me, do we really want buttered brack with our salmon?" He went across to the sideboard and removed the covers from the dishes. "Hot potato cakes? Bacon, eggs and black pudding? This is not what I ordered for dinner, Maggie or Bridie."

"If you please, then, Mr. Thomas, it's not dinner at all, it's tea," Maggie or Bridie revealed. "The cook was saying, you didn't get tea, and you'd have to get tea before you got dinner."

"An orderly mind," said Mr. Buckle.

Miss Boxham bridled.

"When will dinner be?" Thomas asked. "If we eat this up, like good people, will it follow at once?"

Maggie or Bridie tossed her head. "Indeed, I cannot tell you that. The cook is too great to diminish herself explaining to the likes of us."

"Will you ask her from me, what are her plans?"

A mulish look came over the woman's face. "I'd hate to disappoint you, Mr. Thomas, but we don't be conversing."

"Already!" Thomas gravely shook his head. "And the creature has hardly unpacked her things!"

"It was better she didn't unpack them at all, for she'll never suit," his henchwoman averred. "What with cooking for a monsignor before she came here, and being born and reared on the mainland, she thinks she's the Queen of Sheba. I declare to you, Maggie and me's disgusted."

Miss Boxham was ready to weep with mortification. The way of life appropriate to the quality seemed impossible to achieve: everything always turned to farce, and bad farce into the bargain. It was diabolical. Moreover, she could see that Mr.

Buckle was greatly enjoying the fun. No doubt it corresponded to absurd, fallacious ideas of the country he'd picked up before he came, and now he'd write back in triumph to say it was all he had expected. She writhed with shame at the thought, and inwardly raged against her brother for not writhing too.

He was, in fact, wholly unshaken. "Well then, Bridie, we'll make the best of it," he said. "Bring us some tea and then you can go. I'll have a word with the cook later on."

"What did I tell you?" he twinkled at Harry as the woman left the room.

Miss Boxham could not allow this to pass. "What *did* you tell him?" she asked frigidly. "I hope, that you hadn't a notion in the world how to choose your staff."

"Choose!" said her brother, laughing. "Choose between what?"

Miss McGrath, the lady from the mainland, had in truth been the only postulant for the job. She was the latest in a long stormy succession, each of whom had left her mark on the Boxham annals. Just as one forebear had planted the wood and deepened the lake, another added to the house itself, another embellished the gardens or founded the library, so one cook had set the kitchen on fire, another sold off the fruit of the orchard, another privily installed her brats in the hayloft. Their crimes were many, their virtues few or none, but each had appeared, at the time, to be the likeliest of the candidates offering.

"Hers is a very noble concept of tea," said Mr. Buckle pacifically. "I am extremely fond of bacon and eggs, and everyone admires your potato cakes. Black pudding is rather beyond my experience."

"It would probably make you ill," Miss Boxham assured him. "We peasants eat anything."

"Stop pecking at the poor chap, Sabby," her brother commanded. "What the divil's he done to deserve it?"

It was what all the Mr. Buckles were rather than what they did that set Miss Boxham off; but she saw the injustice of holding them responsible for that, and she now made an effort to speak kindly to this particular specimen. He went more than halfway to meet her, and managed so ably that before the meal was ended she was half won over. His appreciation of the exotic viands and the rank tea, which came out of the dented aluminum pot with the milk and sugar already added, could hardly have been a pretense; and his manner implied that the whole affair, far from being a stroke of Irish quaintness, was but normal practice in the world of today, unlikely to arouse comment in Windsor Castle itself.

With everything so pleasant, Sabina determined not to have the private talk with Thomas for which she had applied, but to broach matters frankly in the presence of Mr. Buckle, hoping to find him an ally.

"I have come to ask a favor," she began, as they were sitting out in the garden after tea. "And please don't say no at once before you have thought it out."

"As if I would!" murmured Thomas, who was again lying back with his eyes comfortably shut.

Sabina then proceeded to give him an account of the Action Committee's plans, laying stress on the benefit to the island could they be successfully carried out. Apart from expressing the hope that he would not be called on to play the Saint, her brother listened without a word, but when she came to the crux of her mission, he opened his eyes in amazement.

"Here?" he echoed. "Have the thing here? You can't be serious."

"Of course I am serious, Tom," she retorted. "It is the ideal setting for a pageant of this kind. It could have been made for it."

"But it wasn't," he dryly pointed out. "And I'm having no rabble in here, foreign or native."

Sarah heaved a weary sigh: her brother's reactionary outlook was another source of affliction. "Who said anything about rabble? Is it the rabble that goes to Oberammergau time after time and makes it world-famous?"

"Oberammergau?" Thomas gave a low whistle. "I fear that, as Nanny used to say, our eyes are a little bigger than our tummy."

"Why will you always be so crushing?" she asked in a tired way. "Ireland is one great reservoir of talent. Everyone agrees on that."

"I don't know who everyone may be, but there's precious little to show for it." Thomas had closed his eyes again and was apparently composing himself for slumber.

"A fine way to talk in front of a stranger!"

"There's nothing strange about Harry. We were at school and Corpus together."

The reference to his alien education, as if it were the most natural thing in the world rather than proof of her father's own disloyalty, flicked Sabina on the raw. "Oh, Thomas, you know what I mean," she said hotly. "I call it fouling your nest. Why must you slap poor little Ireland, with an Englishman here?"

"Ireland was one great reservoir of talent a second ago," said Thomas drowsily. "Wake me up when you've decided which it's to be."

"She needs help, advice, encouragement, leaders, if she's to realize herself," Sabina informed him, and her fine hazel eyes grew moist as she spoke. "Don't you feel any sort of obligation towards her—your native land?"

"No," replied Thomas, his promptitude showing he had given the matter some thought. "None whatsoever."

Mr. Buckle had been following this exchange with some disquiet, and he seized the chance now offered of introducing another topic.

"What can this vehicle be?" he inquired, as a van full of pots and tins and brooms drove out of the rhododendron tunnel and made for the house, rattling and clanking.

Thomas reopened his eyes with a patient air, as if the calls upon them tonight were unduly heavy. "That is Murphy's traveling shop," he said. "And it is also the local taxi. I have no need of either."

The shop, or taxi, drew up at the side, or kitchen, door, and its hooter emitted a series of croaks and gurgles. Presently a squat figure in black appeared, carrying suitcases which she dumped on the ground. Having indicated by a lordly wave of the hand that the vanman could stow them aboard, she retired whence she had come, to re-emerge with a number of brown paper parcels. These and the cases being finally, after discussion, ranged to her approval in the body of the van, she mounted the cabin with immense, affronted dignity and was noisily borne away.

"There goes the cook," said Thomas with the resignation of

(37)

long experience. By occult island methods, Maggie and Bridie had contrived to expel the foreign body in their system. "Now we'll never know when dinner was to be. Nor what she would have made of the salmon." He closed his eyes again.

"You should never have taken a priest's housekeeper," Sabina said. "They are always too big for their boots."

Thomas reminded her that there had been no choice in the matter. The discussion turned on the impossibility of finding people to do things nowadays, and the slum conditions that resulted. Sabina seemed to have forgotten her brother's refusal to help with the pageant. Her moods changed as fast as the island weather, and she now embarked on a lively account of the bathtub—high, dry and useless on her lawn—and the missing taps. She dwelt on Shamus' role in the drama with an irony she would have rebuked in anyone else. As the shadows began to lengthen and a breeze sprang up, she went for her pony and started for home.

"Well, there is something to be said for the place," Thomas called after her. "I needn't warn you not to speak to any strange men. Not even the tinkers. They have just arrived on the prowl, I hear, being no great followers of the press and thus unaware that we are an island. My woods will be spared from now on."

"Well, I think it is a great pity, that's all."

For a stirring sight they made, the tinkers, with their gay wagons, the skewbald ponies running free alongside, the shawled women, bright-eyed and hard-faced with stolid babies on their lap, the lurchers nosing hungrily here and there as they followed in the train. Sabina hated to think of the authorities' efforts to end their wild poetic existence and mew them up in settlements and schools.

"I am sorry about the cook, Harry old boy," said Thomas as they went indoors. "It is lucky that you like rashers and eggs, for that's about all Maggie and Bridie are good for. Heigh-ho! In Ireland, you laugh or go mad. I choose to laugh. What my sister has chosen, you may judge for yourself."

"Miss Boxham laughed too, several times," Mr. Buckle observed. "And looked very nice as she did so."

Four

SABINA'S HOUSE was a long, low whitewashed cabin, formerly owned by one of the numerous tribe of Fizelles, whose family after his death had moved across the water. In building on, she had seen to it that the old, simple lines were preserved: she had kept the stone hearths, flagged floors and high timbered ceilings that gave each room a peasant quality and made it an icebox in winter. It had cost a great deal of money, what with the Dublin architect and the imported labor, but she felt she was living as one of the people. They, on the other hand, spoke with interest of her silver, glass, china, rugs, books, pictures, bath and water closet.

That night, after the visit to her brother, she lay in bed dreamily gazing through the window and thinking how delightful a place it was. The mountains of the mainland were velvety black against the sky, and the moon had cast a shimmering band of silver across the sea. The little waves broke crisply on the shore and rolled lazily back, fizzing, over the shingle. Now and again there was a splash as a salmon leaped, or the snarling whine of a fox, or the call of some nocturnal bird, and lulled by these familiar sounds, she soon was fast asleep.

In the early hours she was awakened by a tremendous clap of thunder. A freak storm had blown up out of the clear sky, as it was apt to do in warm weather. Then there came a brilliant flash overhead and almost simultaneously an explosion in her sitting room, followed by a fierce stutter from the telephone. Oh, not again, not again! Every time there was lightning, the telephone was knocked out, every time there was a gale, the electric current went off, and a couple of days might pass before they were restored. Sabina wearily made her way next door and picked up the receiver. It stuttered more wildly than ever, with the vehemence of a machine gun, and she slammed it down. On the window sill behind it was a Guinness bottle containing holy water, the gift of a friendly neighbor, for use in emergencies like the present and any others that might arise. Many a time she had drawn the attention of her visitors to it, as an instance of the beautiful, simple faith to which her people clung; now, with a fretful mutter, she hurled it into the rubbish basket and retired to bed. The storm raged and the telephone crackled for another hour, and then both suddenly held their peace. Sabina fell asleep again, and did not wake until the sun was already high. After the storm the whole country was a-smile, with a look of beaming innocence, but the telephone was dead as a doornail.

With diabolical precision, this always occurred when she particularly wanted to use it. This morning had been earmarked for a showdown with the Ballycagey laundry. Half a dozen letters to that enterprise had elicited only the assurance, in ladylike writing on paper with a crest and the motto *Nil desperandum*, that the matters complained of were receiving attention. These matters were sufficiently grave. It was quicker and safer by far to get three men to the moon and back than to send a couple of sheets to the local wash. Her finest linen pair, with pillow slips, had been in orbit for over eight months. A white batiste blouse had returned with a new bold pattern in what seemed to be tar. In place of some riding breeches, evidently lost, the laundry kept trying to fob her off with a pair of old serge trousers, patched on the seat with material of a different kind. Every week she posted this garment back, with a firm disclaimer of ownership, and week after week it reappeared, in her parcel and on her bill.

Up to now she had not resorted to the telephone, because of the difficulty of getting through to the management. The business belonged to an order of nuns whose Mother Superior believed that no good ever came of contact with the outer world: if people rang up, they either got no answer at all or found themselves in touch with the convent gardener. But on receiving the ragged trousers for the sixth or seventh time, Sabina had resolved to bear it no longer. She was going to call, for hours if need be, until she got a reply, nor did she mean to hang up until she had spoken to someone in charge. That was to have been her morning's work; and now, like most things planned or premeditated on Inishnamona, it had fallen through.

She was halfway through her breakfast when she heard wheels on the road and a rough voice bidding an animal stop. One of the tinkers from the encampment must have ventured across on the ferry after all. He was a big, rawboned fellow with a mop of ginger hair, a bedraggled wife and two dirty children, all with faces that seemed to be carved from wood. A donkey was tied to the rear of his cart. The tinker got down, pushed the gate open and advanced upon the cottage, while the woman sat grinning and looking on.

Sabina smiled pleasantly as she opened the door. It was the first time that tinkers had ever stopped at her place—why, she did not know, but they invariably passed her over. People said they left some mark on every gate to let others know if, from their point of view, it was a good house or a bad, but they merely drove by hers without turning their heads, as if it didn't exist. This departure from custom was quite a surprise, and the conversation that followed was another.

"Are you the woman of the house?" the tinker demanded roughly, and without waiting for a reply, he went on, "Have you any old lamps, pots or scrap metal?" Now he put a hand on the doorway to prevent Sabina from closing the door.

It was hardly what she expected, her ideas of tinker speech being drawn from romantic writers of the Celtic Movement.

"I'm afraid not," she said.

"Are you sure of that?" He looked over her shoulder into the room beyond, his eyes flitting rapidly to and fro as if he had come to make an inventory. "The candlesticks, what about them?"

The four heavy silver candlesticks he stared at so greedily were a bequest from her grandmother. Whether he had an inkling of their value or simply coveted them for their size and weight Sabina could not judge, but it was plain that he seriously thought she might hand them over.

"There's nothing at all I want to dispose of," she answered shortly.

"Buy the ass of me, then!" He jerked his head toward the cart in the roadway.

"Thank you, I don't need an ass."

The tinker threw her an angry look, as much as to say his patience was wearing thin. "What'll ye do for me, so?" There seemed no question in his mind but that she must do something. "Them yonder is my young ones, and another coming."

"I'll give you some milk, with pleasure,'" she told him. "And you can have bread and cheese, if you like."

"Milk! Bread and cheese!" cried the man in disgust. "I want money." Then he was off on a different tack, lowering his voice and forcing an expression of piteous appeal. "Ah, why wouldn't you take the poor little ass from me?" he whined. "He's strong as a bull, and hardly three years old."

The ass's head hung down, as if for very shame to hear him. With its dull, sticky pelt, sagging spine and hooves that curled up as if fitted with skis, it looked to be more or less moribund.

"But I don't want an ass, I'm telling you. Now, will I cut you the bread and cheese or not?"

"Okay, missus, okay," said the tinker humbly. "I'll not forget it to you. She'll give us bread and cheese," he shouted to the family in the cart.

"God bless her for it!" the woman shouted back, with a wider grin than ever.

Sabina shut the door and went to the kitchen, moved by this grateful response. That was how tinkers spoke in the plays and stories she read. No doubt it was the dire need of his children that had caused the poor man's rough behavior at the outset, and she would not hold it against him. She cut slices of fresh brown bread, buttering them freely, and hunks of cheese, and parceled them up with tomatoes and apples. Then she poured a pint of ale into a container, which she decided to let the tinkers keep.

Warm with benevolent feeling, she was about to carry the things outside when, through the kitchen window, she saw the cart driven off. The tinker, standing up and yelling, lashed his nag to a gallop while the woman shook her fist at the house and the donkey stumbled along in tow. Something must have occurred to change their unaccountable minds; it was a pity for the wasted effort and the spoiled bread, but Sabina was more puzzled than indignant.

She finished her breakfast and went out to the barrel for water. Two of the neighbors were standing in the road, contemplating her vegetable garden and passing remarks under their breath. Miss Boxham's vegetables were a perennial source of wonder to the people thereabouts. She was not content, as they were, with potatoes, carrots, onions and cabbage. She also grew peas, beans broad and runner, broccoli, radishes, lettuce, artichokes and asparagus. Within the last few days the asparagus had begun to shoot and probably the women were wondering, as they did every year, what those purple points might signify and what in the world they were used for. Every year Sabina explained this, and now, patiently, she prepared to explain it again.

"A glorious day, thank·God!" she called out.

"Indeed, thanks be to God and His Blessed Mother," replied Julia Fizelle, the donor of holy water, in a hesitant way.

The women looked at each other and then at the garden again.

"Miss Boxham, dear," murmured Julia, "did you see your ridges?"

"Ah, don't tell me the cows were in them!"

At this time of year the sweet grass was short, and cows were turned adrift to forage along the road. With legs tied together, they hobbled far and wide, helping themselves to all that took their fancy. As the women made no reply, Sabina put down her pail and hurried to see for herself. Row after row of young peas and beans were torn up and withering in the sun, while heavy boots had kicked and broken the early spears of asparagus.

"The tinkers!" she cried, aghast.

"Now, there's the shocking crowd!" said Bridget Fahy with relish.

"I was getting them food in the house. They must have done it then. But why?" she asked, staring at the wreckage.

"It isn't food they look for," Bridget said. "Them ones are better off than the Lord Mayor of Dublin. If you offer them food, they're only offended."

"But why should they do this to me? Why did they come here at all? They never stopped at the house before."

"They wouldn't stop here, and you with the phone," said Bridget, expounding as one long familiar with these matters. "You could ring the Guards if they were cheeky, and then they'd be cot when they tried getting off the island. But they'll have heard along the road today how all the phones is out of order. Oh, they're cute enough!"

"There's nothing about us they wouldn't know," Julia confirmed. "The house that has a man in it, the house where he's gone to England. All that scares them is men and dogs. You should keep a dog, Miss Boxham."

But Miss Boxham was still in mourning for Pip, the golden Labrador.

"Well, I'd better get on and sort this," she said despondently. As a rule the island could expect piercing winds or savage hailstorms up to the middle of May, but the weather had been kind this year and her crops were well advanced. "It's dry for sowing, all right, and I can't spare a drop of water."

The women now asked her to show what she put in the ground to bring up plants like those that lay scattered about. They were examining the hard yellow peas and the shiny pink beans, mottled with black, when a car came over the brow of the hill and they transferred their attention to that. Julia felt sure it belonged to the doctor, who was after getting a new one. Bridget said it must be owned by the Rector's aunt, down here on a visit and no end of a duchess. Then why would she come this way, Julia wanted to know, instead of traveling the roads put down by the Council? Bridget declared that the likes of them wouldn't know what the Rector's aunt might do, and as for himself, he was gone to one of the islands to help with a baby. That baby wasn't to come for another three weeks, Julia fought back. They argued to and fro until they were out of breath and the splendid car was upon them.

"A stranger!" they muttered in unison as Harry Buckle stepped out. The morning was full of suspense and excitement. Politely they retired, hovering about the car for a while and frequently looking back as they went their way.

"Good morning, Miss Boxham, got you in one," Buckle said cheerfully. "Sharp of me, as your brother's directions were far from clear. I have been sent to fetch you, if you have no other plans."

The Quiet End of Evening

They were to call, it appeared, on Colonel Sentence. A barefoot boy had arrived with a note from him, urging Thomas to come as soon as he could on a matter of great importance—of such importance, indeed, that he could not put it in writing for fear it might fall into enemy hands. *Burn this when read,* the note had concluded. Thomas had flatly refused to undergo a tête-à-tête with the Colonel and would only see him if Sabina came too.

"How like Thomas!" she grumbled. "Why should I put myself out? He will do nothing for me. And what difference will it make if I come or not?"

"He says you're so good with the gallant Colonel," Mr. Buckle explained. "It's like a native charming a cobra. And he declines to go without you."

Thomas had also decided that she was to return with them to Mount Skellin, where she would cook the salmon for lunch; in disposing of other people's time he could always think fast and clearly. Mr. Buckle, however, had instructions to say nothing of this for the present.

"I daresay, all very well. There's heaps to do here. Look at my plants!"

He was already looking. "Enemy action," he observed. "Whom do you suspect?"

"Oh . . . it was only some mischievous boys." The faint, becoming color crept into her face as she told the preposterous fib. Mischievous boys, indeed! There wasn't a boy in the village. The year she came there were five, demons every one. At Halloween they tore up her winter cabbage and threw the leaves about, then knocked at her door, begging for apples and nuts. She well remembered their bright, wicked little faces, and now they were all in England, at work. But she could not bring herself to say who the real culprits were, lest her brother hear of it and gloat.

"Teen-age vandalism," sighed Mr. Buckle. "Evidently universal. But I see you have more to put in," he went on; "do please let me do it for you. It won't take long, and then, perhaps, we could go back for Thomas? He's really dying to know what the Colonel wants him for."

He raked up the plants and set new rows with the brisk, capable movements of much practice. Sabina looked on, abashed to think of her cutting response to his offer of help the evening before. Of that, however, he seemed to have no recollection, nor of the other discourtesies that she had showered upon him; his manner was easy, unconstrained, as if they had been on the best of terms from the start. Reared in a place where nothing was ever forgiven, she felt out of her depth and, accordingly, hostile. As he worked away, pleasantly chatting, she sought relief in ridicule, that favorite Irish specific. Yesterday he had worn a dove-gray suit with a printed shirt that was fine enough for a star. Today he was all in blue, linen jacket and trousers, cotton shirt, flowing silk cravat. Had he a trunkload of fancy get-ups, one for every day of the week? Let him wait till he had to parcel them up and post them to St. Brigid's Peerless Laundry—and better still, till he got the parcel back and saw what was in it! The old serge pants, it might be, or the huge pink woolen bloomers that bobbed up now and again, or a dozen clerical collars. Picturing the scene, she turned away to hide her amusement.

"I have nearly done," Mr. Buckle pleaded, putting this down to impatience.

"Oh, there's time enough. But I'll just put the cob in the field if we are going out."

(50)

Presently they were in Mr. Buckle's car, which was wholly unlike the vehicles Sabina was used to: the engine hummed rather than coughed or stuttered, the doors opened and shut without effort, the gauges and meters were in apple-pie order, the windshield shone. It was unnatural, inhuman, how everything worked as it was intended to do, leaving no scope for ingenuity or improvisation, and it was dull with nothing to bear in mind: no caprices of steerage, no refusal of brakes to act, no seats that fell back and tipped you head over heels.

"Some of our Irish boys will have helped to make this motor," she asserted. "England's industry largely depends on them."

"I am sure of it," was the pacific reply. "But this particular car is a Volvo."

"And is a Volvo so very special?" she demanded with quick belligerence.

"Not at all. But it's made in Sweden."

Sabina was quiet for a moment or two, digesting this information, and then she attacked again. "If I had a car, I would want an Irish one. A Volkswagen, for instance."

"An excellent make," Mr. Buckle agreed. "Very good performance. But on the whole I prefer my engine in the front."

Sabina had no idea where else an engine could be and was certainly not going to ask. The rest of the drive to Mount Skellin was accomplished in silence. Thomas was full of complaints when they got there, as a man constantly badgered and pestered, with never a moment to call his own. He had been to all the trouble of getting the hammock out and setting it up and had fully intended to pass the morning in it, and now here was old Sentence on the warpath again, wrecking his schedule without compunction.

"It's time that fellow was put down," he said, "out of mercy to me. What can he want now? And the telephone isn't working —not that he ever answers. Well, let's go over and see. The sooner we're there, the sooner we're back." He climbed into the car and crossly slammed the door. "If his dogs have savaged the postman, I will not intervene. Drive on."

Five

SIMLA WAS THE NAME of the Colonel's bungalow, bestowed upon it by himself. On his retirement, for a couple of hundred pounds, he had acquired a derelict cabin and transformed it into a small Indian-style dwelling. What had chiefly guided him in making this purchase was the terrain. The property stood at the far end of the island, his nearest neighbor being the friendly and harmless Mrs. Tooth, five miles away. Behind it rose a mountain, a large area of whose worthless land was in his possession: before it was a huge sweep of the bog which had given its name to the island. Protected in the rear, commanding the view in front, he was thus secure from attack by all but the most sneaking and treacherous forces, and those were provided for by a palisade, a lavish use of barbed wire and two redoubtable bitches of the bullterrier breed.

While yet some distance off, the visitors could see a commotion in progress beside the gate, and as they drew near, Sabina recognized the tinker family, the couple yelling and cursing and crying for help while their offspring shrieked in terror. One of the bitches had fastened her jaws in the nag's rump while the other baited the ass; the animals were plunging and rearing in panic as the tinker lashed them and the dogs indiscriminately. The Colonel was up on his roof, sitting with folded arms and urging the terriers on.

"Good girl, Snowdrop!" he bawled. "Good lass, Belle. Worry worry worry!"

"I must say," Thomas languidly remarked as Mr. Buckle pulled up, "the old boy does occasionally have the right ideas."

This was said to provoke Sabina, but, unaccountably, she failed to rise.

Now the Colonel saw the newcomers and whistled his bodyguard off. "That's nothing to what you'll get if you ever show up again," he bellowed after the madly fleeing tinker. By a rope ladder fixed to the chimney stack he made his descent, agile as a monkey; then came the sound of bolts being drawn and keys turning on the inner side of the massive gate, and the Colonel was ready to receive his guests. He was a short, spare man with white hair and mustache, brown face, piercing blue eyes and the bandy legs of a horseman.

"Quite thought you were ambushed, Tom," he grumbled. "Been up there on lookout the last couple of hours. Hello, Sabby, me dear. But who's this chap," he demanded, surveying Mr. Buckle with a frown. "One of the Beatles?" For the Colonel was always a little behind with his information.

"This is Harry Buckle. He's all right," Thomas assured him. "An Englishman."

"Doesn't look all right to me," the Colonel retorted. "The English are a pretty rum crowd these days. What's he doing out here? Wants to stop a bullet, does he? If I were you, young man, I'd scappa," he proceeded, addressing Mr. Buckle, who politely bowed. "Very unhealthy neighborhood, this. We were all but blown to buggery the other day."

"Seven months ago," Thomas amended.

"That's what I said. The other day," the Colonel replied impatiently. "Well, bring your Beatle or Buckle in, but remember, the lot of you, what you are going to hear is *most secret.*" And having welcomed them in these terms, he led the way indoors without further ado.

The room they entered was spotlessly clean but sparsely furnished, with the mounted head of the Colonel's first fox, leering down from the wall above the fireplace, as the single ornament. On the mantelshelf, however, was a crowd of photographs depicting horses, hounds, polo ponies and brother officers, and on the writing desk, the studio portrait, framed in silver, of a beloved mare, long dead.

"Sorry there's nothing to drink," the host said gruffly, pulling up some kitchen chairs. "It's on order, but the fellers here are so bloody slack about delivering." He invariably produced this formula, although everyone on Inishnamona knew that liquor never entered the house, and precious little food apart from the terriers' rations.

Whatever Thomas might say, it was untrue that the Colonel frequently applied to him for help or advice. The explosion had brought him to the house in a hurry, but everyone, on that fateful night, was rushing to and fro. The previous occasion had been

(*55*)

a couple of years before, when the Government circulated a booklet on the procedure to follow in case of an atomic attack. It was written in Irish, hence unintelligible to all but a bare half-dozen, but it was freely illustrated with cartoons of people driving their beasts under cover, cowering in shelters themselves or administering a rough-and-ready first aid. The Colonel leaped to the conclusion that it was some devilry of the IRA. Anything in Irish was apt to have this effect, even the annual notice that his rates were due. Like the gallant officer he was (M.C., D.S.O., mentioned in countless dispatches), he sped to Mount Skellin with a closely reasoned plan of defense, in which he and Thomas would sell their lives as dearly as they could, reserving their last two bullets for Sabina and Mrs. Tooth. As a general thing, however, he lived alone with his premonitions, confiding in no one but Snowdrop and Belle; but the years passed so quickly and uneventfully here that Thomas had an impression the Colonel was in and out all the time.

But clearly, today, whatever might be on his mind, it was not the republican peril. "Just a moment, till I open the safe," he said, with an air of suppressed jubilation. "There's something inside that will make you sit up."

He twisted and turned the knobs on a steel safe, which took up a third of the room, until the door swung back, revealing a litter of boxes, files, balls of string, bottles of ink and glue, a revolver and the skeleton of a cobra. From a place of concealment behind these treasures he drew forth a tumbler of liquid, colorless but for a faint iridescence floating on top, and this he handed to Thomas with the simple command: "Try it!"

"Is it potheen?" Thomas inquired, with no great enthusiasm.

"Try it," barked the Colonel, drawing his snowy brows together above his fierce blue eyes.

Thomas obediently took a sip and screwed up his face in disgust. "Ugh! Look here, dash it!"

"There!" Colonel Sentence crowed in triumph. "Now d'ye see what I'm getting at? Hey what?"

"I cannot say I do," Thomas replied. "It's very nasty, that's all." And he put the tumbler from him with a sulky expression.

The Colonel leaned forward and tapped him portentously on the knee.

"That water came out of my own little stream," he said. "The pitcher I used was clean as a whistle. Do you really fail to appreciate the significance of the flavor?" He paused for this to sink in, and then continued dramatically, *"There is oil on this island!* How much, exactly where, we cannot at present come at. It is a question for experts, which is why, until it is fully explored, not a word of this must be breathed to a soul. Or the local hooks'll have it before you'd say Knife. But I'm pretty sure it's somewhere on my land. Oil!" he murmured dreamily. "Oil! Why, we may become a second Arabia!"

"I should have thought that one was plenty," Thomas objected. "Do we really want a bunch of oilmen mucking us all about?"

"I should move," the Colonel frankly avowed. "With the royalties, I should take a place in Meath and keep a racing stable. I'd run me own pack, what's more. It would be life again, instead of this bloody stagnation. Just to think of it makes me feel ten years younger."

"It could certainly bring prosperity to the island," Sabina

said doubtfully. "But it seems a fearful price to pay."

Already she saw her country's beautiful face pitted with wells and bristling with derricks, shantytowns arising, hordes of strangers bursting in.

"Why did you wish to see me, Colonel?" Thomas then asked. "How can I help you?"

"With advice," was the prompt reply. "I'm out of my depth in commerce. With us, it's always been land or the Army. Thought I could pick up a wrinkle from you."

This delicate allusion to the Boxham ancestry caused brother and sister to exchange a glance.

"Well, the first thing is to send a sample of the water up to the relevant department in Dublin, I suppose," Thomas said. "But won't you wait a little while first? It may run clear again, and then it's all for nothing."

But the Colonel refused even to consider delay. "What if it does run clear?" he demanded. "It was clear before. It comes from a spring high up in the mountain and trickles straight down to this house. Only a turf track crosses it somewhere, and I believe it goes under that. Pollution is out of the question. No, the oil in that water came from the ground itself!"

He was so positive about it and so happy in his dream of the future that the Boxhams forbore to argue. Mr. Buckle had sat in silence throughout, blinking a little like an owl in sunlight. The Colonel made a few last inquiries about the procedure he should follow, bound them all to secrecy again, thanked them for coming and told them to go.

"Must give the girls their tiffin," he said. "Eh, my pretties?"

The pretties flung themselves upon him, yelping approval,

as he restored the precious fluid to its place.

"Mad as a hatter," said Thomas as Mr. Buckle started the car. While they were still with Colonel Sentence, his own burning conviction had had some effect, but now, away from those hypnotic blue eyes, reason asserted itself. "And he might have broken the news differently. I can taste the filthy stuff yet."

"He wanted you to feel the discovery in all its force, as he himself had done," Mr. Buckle suggested. "Now, which is our road?"

It was decided to go back by a different route, making the tour of Inishmamona. There was time enough before lunch, for the bell of the little monastery was just then ringing the midday Angelus. Their way ran through the mighty bog, purple-brown in the sun with low black cliffs where the turf had already been cut; here and there lay pieces of bog oak, fantastic in shape, thrown up after centuries of burial, or a splendid pair of curving horns, all that remained of a ram. The car bounced on the springy road as if on rubber; the people cutting and spreading on either side paused in their work and waved as it passed them by. High overhead the larks were singing as if dear life depended on it; below, the sea stretched away never ending, shimmering gold near the shore, dazzling blue farther out, a purple band on the horizon.

"I feel as if I were on a revolving stage," Mr. Buckle said presently. "Surely that is the Colonel's bungalow again, down over there?"

"Yes. The place is rather confusing like that, we've made a loop," Sabina explained. "Now, you see that ruined cemetery on the side of the mountain and the track that runs past it?" The track curled up and out of sight, a pale ribbon against the somber brown, as if someone had started to peel a potato but changed his mind. "In the old days when a person died in the village beyond, the neighbors carried the coffin on their shoulders to it every inch of the way. Now they have Milo Twomey's hearse," she concluded, with a sigh for the appealing customs of yore.

"Who is Milo Twomey?"

"The dacentest man that ever trod leather," Thomas said with ironic inflection.

"The local tycoon," Sabina said frostily. "With a finger in every pie. You can't even get buried without him."

"Well, I think I would settle for Twomey's hearse if I were a neighbor," said Mr. Buckle, gauging the distances. "Hello, what's going on up there?"

"Where? Nothing. It's never used now."

"Someone is using it today, however," said Mr. Buckle. "And someone appears to be in trouble."

Six

FAR ABOVE, a white object was waving about in frantic sema-
phore. It looked no bigger than a pocket handkerchief, nor, at
that distance, could anything else be seen, but the movements
were such as could only be meant for a signal.

"We must go and find out," Sabina declared at once.

Thomas heaved a sigh. "Two incidents in one morning,"
he complained. "And to think I was quite resolved to spend it
in the hammock!"

"You would never suppose, would you," Buckle asked of
Sabina, laughing, "that at Oxford your brother was regarded
as a human dynamo?"

"The west of Ireland is very relaxing," Thomas replied.
"Well, do as you wish, my dears, but expect nothing from
me."

Buckle skillfully reversed the car up a narrow lane dividing two plots of bog, and drove to the foot of the track. "I be-

lieve we can make it," he said. "And I just hope we do, for I can't see anyone towing us down."

He went up slowly, weaving from one side to the other, avoiding a gully here, a boulder there. The car behaved like a thoroughbred, although never intended for operations such as this. After a while, as she rounded a bend, the occupants saw the figure of a woman, dressed all in white with a long train, holding in her hands what they realized, a little farther on, was a bridal veil. A short distance below her, on the hillside, lay the body of a man, unconscious or dead, and about fifty more yards below that was a car with its wheels in the air, apparently a total wreck.

Now the woman caught sight of the rescue party, and throwing her veil on the ground, stumbled toward them on precariously high heels.

"You're Philomena Roche, are you not?" Sabina asked with much concern. She vaguely remembered that one of the rare local weddings was to have taken place that morning. "What on earth has happened to you?"

"Me da tried taking a shortcut," said Philomena with a burst of angry tears. "Said he knew the way like the back of his hand. The back of me hand to him, that's all! I'm finished with him for good."

"But is it he that's lying out on the hill? He seems to be hurt."

"Is it hurt?" retorted the bride with a fresh paroxysm. "Sure, that's nothing but drink. Him and the boys were at it all night. We started out at half-eight and we're here ever since. He died over the wheel and I had only the time to jump clear before the yoke was down the side, tipping him out and turning over and over, and will you look at it now?"

"We'll get you to your wedding," Sabina consoled her. "We can do it, can't we, Mr. Buckle?"

"Yes, but we'll have to go on. It's out of the question to turn," he said, with his eyes fixed thoughtfully on the vehicle below.

"There you see! Come, dry your eyes and powder your nose till I collect the veil and put it on you. You'll be only a little late!"

Sabina ran for the veil, which, ballooning in the mountain breeze, was on the point of taking off altogether. While she smoothed the creases and restored it to its rightful place beneath a silver-paper crown, Buckle continued his survey of the wreckage. So intent was he that Thomas, curiosity overcoming inertia, got out of the car and came to make inquiries. Buckle pointed to a stream that meandered down the mountainside, passing immediately below the shattered hood.

"Follow the course of that to the end," he directed.

"I haven't your eyes," said Thomas doubtfully, screwing up his own. "But let me try . . ." Then he exploded in a bitter laugh. "Oh Janey Mack!"

The watercourse led to the meager lands of Colonel Sentence.

"The second Arabia," murmured Buckle.

"Everything here begins and ends in tomfoolery," Thomas declared. "I ought to have guessed it all at once."

"I don't see how anyone could."

Further analysis had to be postponed, as Sabina was now escorting the bride to the car. Miss Roche's nose had caught the sun and she had left her powder behind, but her bridal attire was sumptuous. It had been the admiration of all for the past decade, biding its time in Twomey's between the fishing rods and the

Souvenirs of Ireland, and now, filled by Miss Roche to capacity, looked more impressive than ever.

Leaving her senseless parent to dry in the sun, they set forth on their journey. As they jogged and jolted upward, the reconstituted Philomena talked nineteen to the dozen, as if her tongue had shaken loose. Her feet were killing her, she said, her shoes were a fright. It was them and also the fear of looking a Judy, that had kept her grilling there all morning rather than battle down to the road. She wondered would Pat McGinty have waited, or would he flinch from her altogether? Neither he nor she was hot for getting married; their mammies had fixed it up. She had been promised for years to Dano, the postman, but he never would fix the day, only reached for the bottle when the question came up; so now there was Pat, in place of him: a nice quiet boy, no harm at all, only for his wooden leg.

"If I had me pick, I'd go to Manchester," said Miss Roche, stressing the second syllable in local style. "Me two sisters are there before me." But both were married to Protestant English, and Mammy would rather have seen them dead.

By the time they came to the village beyond the mountain, the past history and future plans of Miss Roche were laid minutely bare. But the flow ceased abruptly and gloom set in as they drew up outside the gray pseudo-Gothic church, which seemed, like all the island churches, of disproportionate size. It was nearly two o'clock and not a soul could be seen, either round the door or in the church. The vacant nuptial chairs looked dismal in the empty building. Apart from some drooping calla lilies behind the altar, there was no attempt at decoration. Miss Roche glanced about her glumly and burst into tears again.

The Quiet End of Evening

"This is romance, in the Irish tradition," Thomas muttered to Harry, drawing a frown from his sister.

A lad who had watched their arrival now trotted in and disclosed that the people were gone from it hours ago. They had, it appeared, accepted the position without complaint, except for the mothers-in-law, who had given out something lovely and nearly come to blows. Father Kelly had intervened and taken them off in his car to look for the fugitive—as Mrs. McGinty supposed her—or—as Mrs. Roche's opinion was—the abductee. As yet, he had not returned from his mission. The nuns had shepherded the choir back to the convent, the women were home cooking the dinners and the men had trooped off to the pub in a body.

"They'll never be coaxed out of that," sniveled the bride.

"What'll we do?" Thomas fumed in Buckle's ear. "It's really too bad. We've spent a couple of hours on this nonsense. And I am starving."

Buckle was feeling peckish himself. "I suggest that we all go and take refreshment together," he said. "We cannot abandon the lady on this, the happiest day of her life. Then, if Father Kelly has still not reappeared, you might borrow the car and hunt him, while Miss Boxham and I offer Miss Roche such moral support as we can."

This reasonable proposition brought on another flood of tears from Miss Roche. "I'll not stir! I'll not go out, to be seen like this," she bawled between her sobs. "The neighbors'd die laughing! I'd be the joke of the year!"

"Curious, in this supremely ridiculous land, how sensitive the inhabitants are to ridicule," Thomas drawled.

"Be quiet, you beast!" cried Sabina fiercely.

"Tut tut, my dear Sabby. Remember where we are."

There was little chance, Mr. Buckle thought, of anyone forgetting it. Patiently he put forward a different plan. "Why not take your sister out for a bite?" he said. "First looking in at the pub to reassure the groom. I will keep Miss Roche company here, or perhaps in the sacristy, where she may feel rather more at her ease. If Father Kelly isn't back when you return, an all-out search will have to be made, for as you know, weddings cannot take place after three o'clock. What do you say, Miss Boxham?"

Miss Boxham hardly knew what to say. She had not been aware of the rule in respect of weddings, nor did it matter, since rules were made to be broken, but it disconcerted her to find the Englishman better informed than herself. More disconcerting even than that was his attitude to the whole affair. Along with compassion for Philomena she felt a profound humiliation at Buckle's being there to see it. This, like the fiasco of yesterday's dinner and the lunacy of Colonel Sentence, was what the English expected of Ireland. Their reaction to it was wont to be either amused contempt or, what was equally galling, delighted enthusiasm, as for something too utterly priceless for words. She had been poised and ready to spring at the first appearance in Buckle's manner of either one, but found no occasion to do so. He accepted the situation in a completely unruffled way, threw himself into it, made it his own and looked about for the means of ending it happily. She would never, herself, have thought of Philomena's being more comfortable in the sacristy! His behavior was beyond all criticism and made everything ten times worse.

"I am not hungry, I will stay," she said, then added, with rising color, "but do please call me Sabina."

"Historic moment," her brother observed.

Mr. Buckle was gratified by his promotion but firmly declined her offer to stay. They were arguing to and fro when the case was abruptly altered, just as the local weather would veer from drizzle and fog to radiant sun in a matter of minutes. Father Kelly hurried into the church, a little worn by his strivings with the mothers but with both of them now firmly in hand. News of Miss Roche's mishap had streaked round the island by bush telegraph and caught him up as he was about to abandon the search. He had returned at speed with the ladies, now pacified and in high feather: an edict went forth to the men in the pub; boys ran from house to house calling the women, who obediently cast their aprons aside and resumed their Sunday coats; and the nuns were already under way, bringing the little choristers.

"So dry your eyes and blow your nose," the priest admonished the bride. "Or the people will think it's getting buried you are."

The party from Mount Skellin offered the bride their congratulations and took their leave. On the road they passed the men, somewhat flushed of face and unsteady of leg, making for the church with an air of latent hilarity. The groom himself, denoted as such by a morning coat and a white carnation, was frogmarched along, protesting volubly, by a couple of stalwart friends.

"That's a fine-looking fellow," said Buckle, referring to one of these. He was a magnificent specimen of manhood, tall, broad-shouldered, with a mane of white hair and grave, handsome features, a face to command trust and respect. "He would be just right for St. Patrick, Sabina, don't you agree?"

Touched to find Harry giving thought to the matter, Sabina looked eagerly in the man's direction, but then she gave an indignant snort.

"Why, that's Peadar MacGowan!" she exclaimed. "Who couldn't put my bath in today because he'd to go on the bog!"

Here Peadar caught sight of Miss Boxham and greeted her with a friendly, unembarrassed smile.

"You don't really believe a word they say, do you?" asked Thomas in a weary snarl. Hunger always made him fractious. "Incidentally, how long will it take you to cook the salmon?"

"Cook the salmon? So that's the idea. I might have known it."

"Well, if you prefer, we can go to the hotel."

Sabina was up in arms at once. "Why 'the hotel' in that snooty way, as if there were only one?"

Inishnamona had two hotels, as well as numerous boarding-houses and a whole string of private dwellings, refurnished and recarpeted with the welcome aid of grants made on the understanding that they offer bed and breakfast, although as a rule they were too crammed with relations for this to be feasible.

"There's only one I'd put a foot in," Thomas growled.

"Well, you won't put one there today, for it isn't open," she retorted. "They haven't a single booking so far this year."

"Oh my God!"

"Aha! And when some of us try to do something about it, you won't lift a finger to help."

"Don't start on that!" Thomas begged her. "How long will

it take you to cook the salmon?" he repeated in a tone of pitiful supplication.

"I'm not a bit sure that I'll cook it at all."

"Sabina Boxham!" She was vindictive, really malevolent, like the *tricoteuses* of revolutionary France, knitting away below the guillotine.

"Can we do the pageant at Mount Skellin?"

Thomas cast her a look of loathing. "Why, that's blackmail!" he cried. "I never heard anything so base in all my life."

"Can we do the pageant at Mount Skellin?" repeated the *tricoteuse,* unmoved.

A long, low rumble came from her brother's inside, as if beseeching him to reflect before he spoke. For a moment he wavered, but then a vision rose of howling children and weary mothers, orange peel and plastic bottles and temporary latrines and, crowning indignity, a vote of thanks proposed by Father Kelly to himself and all taking part.

"I must think of those coming after me," he said, very much the *grand seigneur.* "If I allow it once, it will have to be forever. Generations as yet unborn will be saddled with it. Remember how poor James got stuck with the Children of Mary."

He referred to a cousin in County Cork, of whom Sabina was by no means fond.

"All right. You can whistle for your salmon, or cook it yourself."

"Sabina, I would not have expected this, even from you."

His tone was so bitter, so verging on the venomous that Harry Buckle thought it timely to intervene. Although he had been but a week in the country, and less than twenty-four hours on the island, he had already gained a few insights, and, as regarded the pageant, he sensed rather than calculated that it would never take place at all.

"Perhaps the final decision could be left until later," he suggested sweetly. "And I must own, my dear Sabina, that I am rather hungry too."

The laws of Irish hospitality thus invoked, Sabina had no alternative for the present but to give way. "But there'll be no mayonnaise," she muttered.

"How long will it take to cook the salmon?" Thomas inquired yet again, on a note of desperation, as the car pulled up at his door.

"About forty-five minutes," she answered coldly. "All being well."

Thomas greeted these words with a cry of anguish and tore into the house for biscuits and sherry. Sabina made her own way round to the back door, noting outside it the pile of refuse that Shamus had always buried daily, wondering who would perform this task in the future. As she walked down the passage that led to the kitchen, Mother Courage, the semiwild cat, shot past her into the open, a bulky object between her jaws. Bridie and Maggie, as usual at this hour, were drinking tea at the kitchen table, and as Sabina came in, merely looked up with the incurious air of ruminant cattle.

She was not wholly displeased to find that all was far from well, that Thomas must wait even longer than she had predicted. During the brief reign of the cook, the twins had left the Aga range to its own devices. The fire was dead, and when relighted would not be fit for much before the evening. There was a Calor stove for emergency use, but no gas remained in the drum. All that was left was a puny electric ring, on which a pan of water would hardly boil in less than an hour.

But for the presence of Harry Buckle, she would undoubtedly have let things slide. As it was, she put on the water and, after all, set about making mayonnaise. When this was ready, she got out a silver dish, black as all the others, polished it up until it shone and placed upon it a clean linen napkin. In spite of herself, she began to enjoy these domestic preparations. Now she went to the garden for sprigs of parsley to give the salmon a finished appearance. Mother Courage crouched on the wall in the sun, munching away for dear life. Back in the kitchen, the water was on the move at last, beading and twitching, and Sabina added the salt. Then she went to the larder, only to return some moments later with a look of puzzled inquiry.

"Where is the salmon?"

But even as she put her question, the dreadful truth came home.

MEANWHILE THE TWO YOUNG MEN, sitting on the stone balustrade to the front doorsteps, their sharpest pangs of hunger dulled, were deep in a conversation that had continued off and on since Harry's arrival.

"You may think," Thomas was saying, "that today has been no ordinary one. Believe me, that is untrue. All those comic episodes, all that clowning, were nothing out of the way. They are constant, part of the fabric of Irish life. Visitors find it delightfully picturesque and unusual and charming. Me, it drives mad. Could you really stand it, day in day out, year after year?"

"It may be a question of temperament," said Harry serenely. "And also what you ask of life. You clearly have demands which are being frustrated. All *I* want is never to see a board room again. As simple as that."

"But are you prepared to spend your days in nonsense?" Thomas asked. "For it comes to that."

"Since leaving Oxford I have spent every day in nonsense," Harry replied. "Except for a little gardening now and then."

Thomas showed signs of impatience. "How can you talk in that way?" he demanded irritably. "You inherited a fortune with the business and in a very few years you have doubled it. An incredible achievement! How will you get along, when there's no outlet for your abilities?"

"Perhaps I shall find one," Harry said, placid as ever. "Your sister seems to have plenty."

"My sister lives in a dream," Thomas declared, dismissing her with a wave of the hand.

"And up to now I have lived in a nightmare."

An ungainly bird flew up and perched on the telephone wire overhead. Another of the species joined it, and then a third; for a moment they preened and balanced and put their heads together, and then all three went to work, discordantly crying "Cuckoo!" in chorus.

"I have never before seen a cuckoo in the flesh," Harry exclaimed in surprise. "And here are three in a row!"

"You'll see plenty more," Thomas assured him. "This is their own, their native land. And they cuckoo all night as well as all day."

He clapped his hands and the cuckoos flew off, squawking in indignation.

"A cuckoo serenade?" asked Harry. "I look forward to that."

"I fear your case is desperate," said Thomas. "Well, I have done my best for you, as duty and honor obliged me. You still have time to draw back. Indeed, I shall not discuss things further until you have been here a month."

"Be it so."

"And for the love of God, not a word to Sabby!"

"She will have to know sooner or later."

"But not, I beg," Thomas replied with a shiver, "until the Irish Channel's between us!"

"That's all very fine," said Buckle pensively. "But what about me?"

"Carry on as you are. She'll be eating out of your hand before long. Hush, here she is. Lunch must be ready."

Sabina appeared in the doorway, the last person alive, from the looks of her, to eat from anyone's hand. Her face had the grim expression of those who are forced to give pain against their will. Unable to think how to soften the blow, she had decided on making a bald announcement; thus all she said was, "It will have to be bacon and eggs. Mother Courage took the fish."

For a moment her brother was unable to speak. Then he burst into bitter recrimination, reviling her, the cat, the twins and Ireland. "Typical! Typical!" he stormed. "One can't have even a piece of fish. That brute is forbidden the house. Why did those women let her in? What are servants for?" A good deal followed, in similar vein. "I believe they did it on purpose," he concluded, his voice trembling. "They have always pampered that filthy cat."

"That's your doing," Sabina rebuked him sharply. "It was you naming her Mother Courage, after some nun. They think she's special."

"Bacon and eggs will be very nice," said Buckle hastily, fearing another outburst.

But Thomas was a broken man. "Oh, Harry, Harry, just you wait," he said, barely above a whisper. "Just you wait, that's all. You have seen nothing as yet."

Seven

WHEN THE BOXHAMS AND BUCKLE LEFT, Colonel Sentence prepared for Snowdrop and Belle a tiffin of chopped beef, chopped
liver, hard-boiled eggs, mashed carrot and vitamin E, and he was
hungrily watching them wolf it down when a new caller appeared, in the shape of his crony Major Floud.

Of the small enclave of Protestant gentry, only the Major
was English born and bred. He had raced hither after the war,
a refugee from democracy, and settled happily down at once.
What exactly bound him to the Colonel in friendship was hard
to say, for beyond their political views and religious allegiance
they had nothing in common, not even the Army. The Major had
been but a wartime soldier and, properly, ought not to have used
the title; had anyone else done the same, the Colonel would have
vowed him a cad. He was well off and owned the largest property
there, after Mount Skellin, and the Colonel had only his pension.
He was addicted to food and wine; the Colonel was frugal and

Spartan by nature. He read voraciously, if to no purpose; the Colonel scorned to open a book. They both enjoyed magnificent health, but while the Colonel never gave his a thought, the Major lived in constant apprehension, dosing himself, weighing himself, and at the first twinge or sneeze, summoning the doctor at any hour of the day or night. Nevertheless, they were bosom friends these twenty-odd years. Hardly a day went by but one called on the other, and local opinion believed that nothing could ever divide them.

"It's you, is it?" queried the Colonel. "Good. I hope you've had lunch." The mad light shone in his eye again. "I was going to come over presently. Wait till the girls have finished eating and we'll go inside."

"They don't have to worry about the inches," remarked the Major, looking at the iron muscles and taut bellies with envy. "I'm putting on. Farrell doesn't know what he's talking about. A fortnight ago he told me, 'Stick to meat,' and I was fool enough to do it. A whole chicken for lunch and a couple of pounds of steak at dinner, and I haven't lost an ounce. And I can hardly breathe."

"Something terrific has happened," the Colonel continued. "You'll never guess."

"I read somewhere that one should have a grapefruit with every meal," proceeded the Major. "But where the dickens can I find a grapefruit here?"

"Never mind grapefruit. Go for a run before breakfast. There's the sweetie-pies—ready for seconds, are zoo?" The colonel replenished the bitches' bowls.

"Hang it, Roger, you might take an interest."

"Another time," the Colonel decreed. "Anyhow, you eat too much."

"I am eating under medical supervision."

"Then don't eat at all. Best thing." But the Colonel's thoughts were far away.

"Have you drawn a horse in the Sweep, or what is it?" demanded the Major crustily.

The Colonel brushed a possible fifty thousand pounds aside as barely worth considering. "The Sweep!" he echoed, in disdain. "I tell you, it's something terrific."

"Well, don't leave me in suspense. Out with it, man!" the Major cried.

"Hush!" said the Colonel with a hurried glance about him, although the only other beings for miles were Snowdrop and Belle, thoughtfully licking their chops. "Come indoors!" And he led the way at a fast trot to the little room in which he had previously conferred with the Boxhams, locked the door behind him and went to close the window. "You never know who might be snooping round," he said. "Worse than any bazaar."

As the Major did not share this particular phobia, the Colonel's precautions jarred on his nerves. "I hear there's an English lord driving all over the shop in a white Rolls-Royce," he said fretfully. "I came to ask if you knew anything about it."

"There may be, there may be, he hasn't been here," the Colonel replied in an offhand way. "Now! What I am about to disclose must on no account go beyond these four walls. Or I'll be dished before I have started. I had a word with young Boxham but with no one else. He will keep mum, and so must you. I depend on it."

"Yes, yes, by all means," the Major said with mounting impatience. "Just cut the cackle and come to the hosses."

It would have been better, far better, if the Colonel had consented to do so, but once again he would not trust the power of words to make the impact desired. Having topped up Thomas' glass with the filmy liquid in the jug, he passed it to the Major and, as before, commanded, "Taste that!"

"Why?" asked the puzzled Major.

"Taste it, Auberon! Take a good long pull!"

"Is it wholesome?" the Major wanted to know, eying it doubtfully.

"Would I give it to you, were it not?" rasped the Colonel. "Oblige me and do as I say."

The Major saw there was no help for it. Mumbling the glass suspiciously with his lips, like a horse at an unknown trough, he at last collected his courage and took a mouthful. A second later he spat it out with a cry of rage and disgust.

"What have you put in it?" he cried hoarsely, shuddering.

A man may know another intimately for years and years, and yet be unaware of some personal foible, apparently trifling but capable nonetheless of destroying all that bound them each to each. The Colonel was familiar with the Major's fads as a general thing, but he had no inkling of the frenzy aroused in him by food or drink that had been deliberately tampered with, whether by way of a joke or for any other reason. His marriage, which lasted a month, had foundered on this very shore. The bride, a saucy, spirited girl, asked to prepare some planter's punch, had laced it freely with chlorodyne, a compound with an opium base, immensely popular with British troops in the Boer

War. Careless of the vows so recently exchanged, he had bidden her pack and go, and finding him deaf to her representations, she had packed and gone. Now here was his best and oldest friend committing an equally vile and unprincipled act, and he glared at the culprit with all the fury of love betrayed.

The Colonel did not perceive it, having no thought to spare for anything but the matter in hand. He was gratified by the Major's response, for it seemed to show that the point was fully taken.

"Nothing," he said in high complacency. "It came like that from the ground. That is what I wanted to bring home."

"You might have poisoned me," was the fierce rejoinder. "But for my presence of mind, you probably would."

"Do you realize what this means?" the Colonel continued. "I am sending a bottle of it to Dublin today, on Boxham's advice. There can be no doubt whatever that valuable natural resources . . ."

He got no further, for the Major strode from the house and leapt into his car, slamming the door behind him. Mystified, the Colonel threw up the window and urged him to wait, as there was much they had to talk over. But Floud merely started the engine and drove away at high speed, without a word or a backward glance, and with a silent vow never to speak to Roger Sentence again. Whatever the fellow's motive, he was nothing less than a poisoner—a low, sneaking, treacherous poisoner—and among all the villains on earth, to the Major's mind, a poisoner figured as worst. It was by the grace of God that he had found him out in time.

The Colonel thought it a rum go, but could not for the

moment embark on a detailed analysis. If he wanted to catch the outgoing post that day, he would have to look sharp. He sat down at his ancient machine and with two fingers laboriously typed out a letter to the Minister of Natural Resources in Dublin, describing the circumstances of the discovery in full. It was troublesome work, for if he hit a key too hard the carriage hopped a space or two with a kind of snigger, and when he depressed the bar, as often as not the carriage slipped to the end of the line, rattling wildly and ringing the bell. At last, however, he pulled out the completed document, corrected the errors in ink, signed his name, added his rank (Rtd.), put the letter in a double envelope, marking each *Most Secret,* tied the packet round a bottle of the water, placed this in a box with some straw, wrapped the box, waxed the string, addressed it, marked it *Most Secret,* and with a sense of fulfillment, retired to the roof to keep a lookout for Dano, the postman.

When Dano finally hove into view, it was plain from the weavings about of his bicycle that he was under the weather again. The Colonel's bungalow was the last call on his route, the last-but-one being Mollie Mulligan's bar. Here Dano would stick like a wasp in honey, leaving himself barely the time to get to the Colonel and back to the post office before the van collected the outgoing mail at half past four.

This procedure annoyed the Colonel intensely. There was little of urgency in his mail, which consisted of electricity or telephone bills, notices of regimental reunions and bulletins from the Royal Society of British Bullterriers, with now and then a memo from the War Office concerning his pension. But the post office schedule laid it down that Dano should reach his house at eleven-forty and the Colonel desired that he should do so. Again, to his orderly mind, the spectacle of Dano reeling down the path, capless, tieless, tunic and shirt unbuttoned to reveal a furry chest, and fumbling vaguely in his bag for the letters, was a constant irritation.

But nothing, as he knew to his cost, could ever be done. Years ago he had tried reporting him at intervals to the head office of the county, until at last the rumor went round that Dano was to be replaced. To a man, the population was up in arms. Meetings of protest were held, signatures collected, Father Kelly intervened, and a dead cat was hurled into the Colonel's garden. He and only he must bear the blame, it was said, were Dano to starve, along with the four elderly female relations that shared his hearth, and preparations began for a boycott. Never had this indomitable people defended its proud way of life more unanimously or with greater success. No more was heard of replacement, and Dano was drunk for a week.

Some thirty yards from the bungalow the bicycle seemed to tire of its rider, for it halted abruptly and bucked him over the handlebars. As a rule, when this happened, it made the Colonel's day, but as a rule he had nothing of value to entrust to Dano's care. To hand him over that precious bottle was not to be thought of, and it followed that if he wanted to catch the post he must drive to the office himself. Now, he had bought his car second-hand on leaving the Army and it was on its very last legs. The day approached when it must finally expire, and since he could never afford another, the Colonel's isolation would be complete. For this reason he spared it all he could, and the idea of having to take it out because Dano was blotto again fairly made him boil.

He climbed down from the roof and marched to the gate, where he stood with grimly folded arms. Dano had picked himself up and was vainly trying to get back in the saddle. His mind was clearly in chaos, for instead of placing one foot on the near pedal and throwing the other across the hind wheel to the off, he was making feeble attempts, which came to nothing, to throw them both together.

The Colonel watched his capers awhile and barked a terse command: "Stop that fooling!"

"What I'll do then, Colonel, instead?" asked Dano thickly.

"Walk."

Dano obediently staggered along, with the bicycle making figures of eight on the road. As he drew nearer, the Colonel saw that his purple jowl was adorned with a rich black stubble.

"Damn it, man!" he exploded. "Were you too drunk even to shave?'

Dano was of a mild and conciliatory disposition if nobody roused him, but he took great umbrage at that. He had not been too drunk to shave that morning; he had omitted to do so as part of a definite plan. On finishing work, he always repaired to Moriarty's Lounge, the first in a series of calls which took up the rest of his day, and while there the previous afternoon, he had overheard the deliberations of the Action Committee. The defection of his sweetheart, in many ways a relief, had nevertheless caused a gap in his life. Listening to talk of the pageant, he had been fired with a noble ambition to take the role of St. Patrick himself, and he was now growing a beard as a primary qualification.

In the present state of things, however, his powers of thought and expression were unequal to the task of making this clear. "Personal remarks," he said severely," "Is there any need at all for personal remarks?"

"Not if I had you in me regiment," snapped the Colonel, who occasionally forgot that he was no longer in it himself. "A month's punishment with stoppage of pay."

Dano drew himself up and tried to fix his recalcitrant eyes in a quelling glance. "Fine way to talk to Ireland's lashnun ... nanshul saint," he rebuked him. "And with Phila Roche after marrying Pat McGinty!"

"What are you gibbering about?" the Colonel demanded. "Give me the letters and hop it."

"Divil a one for you today," Dano returned with a righteous air. "I was going to tell you, only you didn't let me."

"Pah!" The Colonel wheeled about and stumped away to the garage.

The key was in a hiding place of which no one but himself knew the secret. Not even his friend the Major had been allowed to share it. He never relaxed his vigilance, lest some hook get in and make off with the removable parts of the car. This had recently happened to Mrs. Tooth, who returned from a trip abroad to find her Bentley a mere husk, and the Colonel had no doubt at all but that a similar fate was proposed for his antique Ford.

At the grinding of the key in the rusty lock Snowdrop and Belle rushed forward, shrieking and shivering with joy, hurling themselves on their master and painfully thrashing his legs with their tails. A ride in the car was as much of a treat as a day with the gun, and it was seldom now they had either. They dashed in the second the door was opened and took up their wonted positions in the back seat, each with her nose through a window, and as the car moved off at an arthritic pace along the road they burst into cry. Hearing that dreadful shindy, the people at work on the bog paused to wag their heads and say, "The Colonel's travelin', well."

Thus they came to the post office, where, his humor quite restored, the Colonel handed in the parcel for registration. Then they went home and he sat down to a lunch of bread, cheese and spring onions, with Snowdrop and Belle on the ground at his feet.

"Enjoyed that, didn't you, my lassies?" he said to them. "Well, who can tell? We may be doing it rather more often one of these days. Eh, my lovelies? What do you think?"

His eyes were glowing again. Snowdrop yawned with delight, Belle happily stretched her paws, as they always did when he spoke to them in that tone.

Eight

Two days later, Moriarty convened a special meeting of the Inishnamona Action Committee at the shortest possible notice. He happened to know that Miss Boxham was out, hunting Peadar MacGowan, and he was particularly anxious for her not to attend. This was for her sake, not his; although her devotion to Ireland was never in doubt, when all was said and done she belonged to a certain class, and it was his duty this afternoon to say such things as could only grieve and wound her.

Convoked again so soon and so urgently, the members believed that a favorable reply concerning the grant must already have come, and they hastened blithely to Moriarty's Lounge, eager to know how much there would be and if strings were attached. A glance at the Chairman's face, however, dispelled these hopes at once: his mouth was set and grim and his eyes sparkled with fierce indignation.

"I have asked you here," he began in a tone to match his

looks, "to acquaint you with the insulting remarks that were passed to a highly respected neighbor by a so-called officer and gentleman."

He paused dramatically here for the words to sink in, while the Committee listened agog.

"I'll give it to you plain and unvarnished, the way I had it from Dano himself," he proceeded, "although I hardly like to sully my lips with such talk." And he recounted how Colonel Sentence had called St. Patrick of Ireland a fright and a scarecrow and one that was always too drunk to shave, and said what would happen to him if ever he got in the British Army, with his pay to be stopped and he to be flogged for a month on end. "And aren't they the same today as they always were and always will be?" he concluded on a note of impassioned rhetoric. "The low, dirty, blackguardly landlords!"

For a moment or two the assembly was hushed and still, stunned by the enormity of the offense. Then it burst out all together, buzzing like a swarm of angry bees. The Colonel was compared to Cromwell, Satan and Queen Victoria. His acts of villainy, not least the attempt to ruin a decent public servant and beggar his kith and kin, were recalled one by one. His views on his fellow countrymen, often and freely expressed, were cited, and himself pronounced anathema. And now on top of everything else had come this vile affront to Holy Ireland, in the person of her Apostle: the Committee dwelt on it, squeezing out every last little drop of bitterness, turning it this way and that for shades of meaning with a kind of morbid pleasure, as a man will bite on a painful tooth.

Presently the Chairman rapped on the bar for silence and

asked what was to be done. They had set themselves up as an Action Committee and must prove their right to the name. Rowty Mulligan led off, proposing a boycott; Niall O'Malley wanted the Colonel thrown in the sea, the Christian Brother was all for tarring and feathering. These and many similar notions were debated in turn, and on various technical points rejected. At last they decided to be content with a simple, dignified vote of censure, and after long heated discussion they settled its wording as follows:

> We the members of the Inishnamona Action Committee wish to proclaim to the whole world that we are full of disgust for Colonel Sentence over the cruel, unmannerly and shameless insults he has offered to St. Patrick, our National Saint and Local Celebrity, said remarks being all a pack of bloody lies and you know it. The Action Committee further calls on the Colonel to withdraw his remarks unreservedly and to apologize for same in writing before noon of Friday next. And if you haven't it done by then, take your cow out of Michael Slattery's field or we will do it for you.
>
> *The Inishnamona Action Committee*

The draft, scribbled down on the back of an envelope, was then passed to the Christian Brother for copying in his scholarly hand on a sheet of clean paper. After that, the Chairman invited all present to sign their names; but here he ran against popular feeling.

"Put our names to a thing like that!" cried O'Shea, the contractor. "For the Colonel to know who's in it!"

"He's terrible vindictive, too," affirmed Mick Slattery. "I wish we didn't say whose field he should drive his cow from."

"Ah sure, he would figure that out for himself," said Moriarty. "And what could he do, when all our names were there together? It'll not be nearly so pointed without them."

Mr. Mulligan suggested that Pio Moriarty sign on the Committee's behalf but he refused, not wanting to push himself forward.

"And who's going to bring it to him?" suddenly asked a little man who had been silent up to now. "He's not going to like it at all!"

An uneasy silence followed, each man with a vision of the Colonel on his roof, raking the countryside with binoculars, a shotgun over his knees and the two murderous bitches loose in the garden below.

"We could send it to the Ballycagey *Bugle* and ask them to print it," Mr. Mulligan thought.

"The Colonel would never see it, then," opined the Chairman. "He only reads the London *Times* and all that class of tripe."

"Could we not put it in the post to him, so?" Mr. Mulligan tried again, but his colleagues reckoned that Dano had suffered enough.

For an anxious moment it seemed as if the Committee's blow must fall on space; but then Jerry Maguire hit on a solution as brilliant as sound.

"Here's what we'll do!" he exclaimed, bringing his fist down on the bar. "We'll say the whole thing in the Irish, the way he won't have a clue in the world what it's all about!"

The statesmanlike proposal met with fervent acclaim. The

Christian Brother's services were bespoken once more in preparing a translation, and he knocked it out as follows:

> Is mían linne, baíll Coisde Gníomhartha Inse na Móna, cur i niúl don tsaol go léir go bhuilimíd lán de déistin don Choirnéal Sentence mar gheall ar an masla mínádúrtha, míbhéasach, mínáireach. a thug sé do Naomh Pádraig, ár n-asbal náisiúnta agus ár laoch áitiúil. Níl san méid adúbhraís acht éitheach go tóin síar, agus is maith atá a fhois agatsa é.
>
> Iarraimíd ar an gCoirnéal freisin a chuid focal do shéanadh go neamh-choiníallach agus a leathsgéal do sgríobhadh féna láimh féin roim meadhon lae Dé h-Aoine seo chughainn. Agus muna mbeidh sin déanta agat um an dtaca san, árduig leat do bhó as ghort Michíl Ui Shlatarra, no árdóchaimid féin duit í.

It was agreed by unanimous poll that delivery should be effected by Tomo O'Shea driving up in his van, tossing the document over the palisade and driving off before the bitches got wind of him; and the Chairman, having declared the proceedings closed, begged the gentlemen to try a drop on the house.

"We couldn't take that lying down," he said with complacency, in reply to a vote of thanks. "Mind now, not a word of this to a soul, or Miss Boxham will have our lives." And all pledged themselves to secrecy.

Sabina was very angry indeed when she got the story, a few hours later, from Julia Fizelle. She was quite Irish enough to take nothing on its appearances: realizing, herself, that the Colonel had never made the remarks in question, that they had been trawled in fact from the limitless confusion of Dano's mind, she assumed the Committee members must know it too and were deliberately baiting the man. She was revolted by the meanness of it and also of their going behind her back, and to herself, in the privacy of the heart, she confessed that it was all too like them.

"The Colonel said no such things," she stated flatly to Julia now. "He's probably never heard of St. Patrick. I'll give Moriarty beans for this."

"You'll never let on 'twas I that told you?" cried Julia in panic. "'Tis all a deadly secret!"

"I daresay."

Pio's voice was particularly ingratiating as it came over the wire. "Wasn't I just going to ring you meself," he exclaimed. "I was trying and trying to get you earlier on."

Local etiquette demanded delicacy with regard to falsehood, but Miss Boxham was in no mood to employ it. "You knew I was out," she retorted. "You waved to me as I passed your Lounge. What's this about a meeting?"

"A meeting?" echoed Pio in wonderment, racking his brains to think who the informer might be. "There wasn't a meeting, Miss Boxham. Just a few of the lads dropped in, informal, you know what I mean."

"Then how could you pass a vote of censure?"

Pio was appalled by the very idea. "Nothing was said of a vote, I'll swear to you," he protested. "Only a friendly message there was, and in Irish too, the way he wouldn't misunderstand us."

"Now listen to me, Moriarty," said Miss Boxham, crisp and

cold. "You are surely not such a fool as to believe the Colonel ever said all that?"

Never before had she addressed him in such a tone, nor dropped the "Mr." before his name, and Pio cringed while he took offense. Accustomed to view himself and his actions in the rosiest possible light, he could not conceive of their appearing differently to others. Miss Boxham was merely behaving as he had foreseen she would: dropping her mask, she was ranging herself on the side of her class, of that ascendancy now broken, toothless and out of the game forever, yet still, somehow, to be envied, regarded and feared, for even as these spirited thoughts hummed in his head his spine was curving, he bowed to the telephone as to a living presence and his voice came scared and deferential.

"We had it on the best authority," he pleaded.

"Best authority! That sot?" Miss Boxham's blood was high indeed when she could refer to a paid-up member of the Post Office Workers' Union in such terms. "But do you mean to say you really did believe it?" she went on, more in stupefaction now than in anger.

"Sure, what else could we do?" Pio wailed.

"Then you'd believe anything, that's all. And have you sent this friendly message of yours?"

"I wouldn't have wished it, Miss Boxham . . ."

"That means you have, I suppose. You must go and take it back."

"Ah, wait now, there's the Colonel's dogs, they're desperate, Dano says it's a year off his life . . ."

Miss Boxham hung up without waiting to hear about Dano's

life. She was tired out by the exertions of the day. From one end of the bog to the other she had driven, asking in vain for news of Peadar. At last a cousin expressed the belief that he was up at the lighthouse, sorting a broken window there. On she trotted to the lighthouse at the farthest tip of the island, where the keeper denied all knowledge of broken windows but stated as fact that Peadar was sorting the chimney of the parish house. At this latter point of call, however, Father Kelly declared that he as soon expected the Second Coming. By this time Finn, the cob, wheezed like a kettle from the dust off the road and she turned his head for home, pausing only at Twomey's to inquire about her bath taps; and there in Twomey's yard, she found Peadar himself, painting a signboard for the bar.

Drawing in the reins, she sat awhile and balefully observed him. With languid movements he would touch in a letter, then break off to admire it and refresh himself from a bottle of stout. A little forest of empties stood at his feet, a phalanx of new ones was drawn up on the window sill of the bar; happy, relaxed, from time to time he whistled a jaunty air.

A familiar sense of impotence came over her as she took in the spectacle. Why had she gone to all this trouble? Purely to give herself the illusion of having a part in the direction of her affairs. For Peadar would arrive at her house when it suited his own convenience, and not a moment before. Nevertheless, calling his name, she now demanded with some asperity why he was not there today. Just as she knew he would, just as he always did, he flashed her a beaming smile and replied that he would have been, only that he was prevented. He rose above her manner as if it could only be caused by some private discomfort of her own, unrelated to any doing of his.

"I'll be up to you in the morning, Miss Boxham," he assured her in tones of honey. "That's as true as the bottle of stout in me hand." And he took a pull at the bottle by way of emphasis.

Miss Boxham gave him a look but would not deign to comment. "Hold Finn for me, like a good man,' she said, wearily climbing down from the trap. "Not that he's exactly fresh— we've been all over the world to find you. Your wife thought you were on the bog, why couldn't you tell her where you were going?"

"I didn't know meself till I got here," replied Peadar, whose life in fact was full of these little surprises. "Now, that's a fine animal you have there, Miss Boxham," he went on easily, regarding the other theme as exhausted and stroking the cob's sweaty flank. "He'll win the Grand National for you yet, it wouldn't amaze me!"

In Twomey's Hardware, sandwiched between the bookstall and the Ladies' Millinery, only one of the four assistants was at the moment on active service. Two of the others were deep in a discussion of yesterday's football results, and the fourth was treating himself to a shave with an electric razor from Twomey's stock. With long pauses for cogitation, a farmer was ordering bags of nails, pots of paint, brushes, linseed oil, a bit brace and a statue of the Infant of Prague. Rather than list these items and collect them comfortably all together, the assistant ambled off to find each one as it was named, with slow, heavy movements as if walking under the sea. Miss Boxham awaited her turn, seething and yet resigned, aware that no power on earth could hurry them up. At last the Infant of Prague was swaddled in paper and string, and she moved nearer the counter, where a stout woman in shawl and boots was plainly intending to jump the queue; but the farmer, dragging a spoutless teapot from the depths of his clothing, began a long spiel of how the spout had dropped off of it, just like that, and he only after buying it, and he wouldn't be speaking of the poor little thing but that he knew Mr. Twomey would wish him to get it again. Negotiations were begun and were bound to be protracted, and throwing decorum to the winds, Miss Boxham boldly addressed the two other youths as they sat conversing on a roll of linoleum.

"Are you busy?" she demanded.

They looked up in surprise, at her and then at each other, while they turned the question over in their minds. Apparently they found nothing objectionable in it, for both of them smiled at her in the friendliest way.

"Not too bad," said one, and resumed the conversation.

Having got his shave, the fourth assistant was appreciatively fondling his velvety-smooth lip and jaw. Now he blew some little ginger whiskers off the razor, which he carefully packed in its box and replaced on the shelf. This done, he looked about him with the keen businesslike air of a man with no time to lose, and, his eye falling on Miss Boxham, he greeted her as though she had just come in.

"I'll have to get one of those lads meself, really," he confided, jerking his head toward the razor and caressing his chin once more. "It's handy, all right, shaving here, but there's no privacy in it. Now, what's this I can do for you, Miss Boxham?"

"I called to ask about my bath taps," she said. "Mr. Twomey said the lorry could bring them from Dublin. Do you know when it's next going up?"

A shadow crossed the young man's face and he looked at her

doubtfully, wondering how best to break the news. "The lorry mightn't go so very soon at all," he replied, by way of a first installment.

"I thought it went up twice a week."

"It did, it always did till now. But there's a catch in it since the other day. Is it the ferry master or Mr. Twomey or the insurance crowd itself, but the lorry can't travel be water again, for fear it would all go down."

Miss Boxham was much put out, but not altogether surprised. She had from the first had misgivings about the famous exploit. True, it had briefly focused public attention on the plight of the west. All the Dublin papers carried emotional leading articles on the subject, and the Grand Old Man of Irish letters, Fergus Fahy, had broken a befuddled silence of fifteen years with a two-page spread entitled "I ACCUSE!" But what, in concrete terms, had come of it all? How was anyone in the least better off? The Emporium, for instance, should have been full of strangers this afternoon, buying Irish tweed and knitted garments, exotic tinned foods imported only for them, plaster leprechauns and Celtic jewelry made in Japan, postcards of the island bathed in tropical sunlight and, of course, umbrellas and rubber boots. Instead, there was one English boy, with hair to his shoulders and filthy clothes, vacantly sucking a lollipop, and apart from him, a handful of countrywomen, wandering here and there, asking for small cuts of bacon and slices of processed cheese, quarters of tea and sugar, or simply taking up space while they chewed over their meager bits of gossip. And what was happening in Twomey's merely exemplified, summed up, the fate of Inishnamona as a whole.

The piped music, installed for the enjoyment of the missing tourists, had finished with "Oh Danny Boy" and was embarking on "Come Back to Erin."

"But wait now, Miss Boxham," the assistant said, in sudden recollection, "these same bath taps, didn't I see on the book how the order was canceled?"

"Most certainly you did not," she informed him tartly. "Or you had no business to."

The youth fetched the book, and with much licking of fingers, turned over its grimy pages until he found the entry. "Canceled!" he confirmed in triumph. "Canceled last evening!"

"Who canceled them, pray?" she demanded.

"I couldn't tell you for sure," he replied. "Me colleague Joe made the note. But I presume it would be yourself."

Miss Boxham contained her wrath with an effort. "May I have a word with Joe?"

"You may, of course, only he isn't here. His mother's cousin dropped dead this morning and he'll be out till after the funeral."

"Well, put the order in again and please mark it 'Urgent.' The taps will have to be posted."

She made as if to go, but the youth had not quite reached the end of his story. "While we have the post at all!" he said lugubriously. "There's more lorries than ours taking fright at the ferry, the lads with the petrol and oil, now, they're not coming, and who knows if the post office van won't get the jitters as well? Sure, we'll be worse off than Robinson Crusoe himself."

Come back to Erin, mavourneen, mavourneen! the amplifiers were wailing. Unable to bear any more, Sabina took to her heels.

As she entered the sunlit yard, Twomey's black-and-silver hearse came slowly out of its hiding place for a lick and a polish, in honor of Joe's departed kinswoman. Peadar was painting and swigging, impartially, turn and turn about. Evidently he had tired of holding Finn, who had wandered off and was munching the straw round the legs of a table which, Sabina remembered, had been lying there upside down for the past eight weeks.

And then after all these time- and spirit-wasting *démarches*, which as usual led to nothing, she had returned home to find Julia Fizelle hovering at her gate, full of the vote of censure. Julia was grievously disappointed by her reaction, and puzzled too, since to one of her barren life no news was ever unwelcome or vexatious: it was an absolute good in itself, just as a death was. And it was thanks to the death of that morning that she had picked up the item at all. The regulars from Moriarty's had come reeling up to the dead woman's house in a body and given the Committee away. Julia, who dearly loved a wake, had cut things short, had dragged herself from the pleasant coziness, the murmured prayers and low-voiced talk, the rattle of teacups and clink of glasses, the clouds of cigarette smoke drifting above the little waxy doll of a corpse in her satin robe and frilly bonnet, merely to pass the information on the sooner to Miss Sabina. And far from appreciating her sacrifice, Miss Sabina snapped her head off, tossed the reins of the trap over the gatepost and rushed indoors to the telephone! There was no fathoming the minds of gentry.

Miss Boxham was issuing forth from the cottage again with a brow of thunder.

"You didn't mention me name, sure you didn't?" quavered Julia Fizelle.

"Of course not. Leave me, will you, like a dear woman. I must think what to do."

Finn grabbed her sleeve in his mouth, to remind her that he was thirsty and hungry as well as fatigued. He would have to be watered and fed, rubbed down and rested, before he went out again. By then night would be coming on and it was perilous to drive these roads in the dark, but reach the Colonel she must, poor man. Ever since the explosion he had believed that a native rising was imminent and himself marked out for destruction. A fine tizzy he'd be in, with messages in Gaelic popping into his letterbox! And she could not ring him up to reassure him, as he was unshakably convinced that the wires were tapped by the IRA.

Julia had been slowly retiring along the road, but now turned back. "The gintleman's coming, Miss Boxham," she called. "The gintleman from Mount Skellin, the one that sorted your garden."

A few moments later the Volvo drew up beside her and Mr. Buckle stepped out, hot and dusty but urbane as ever, holding a parcel in his hands.

Nine

Mr. Buckle was unlike any of the young men that Sabina knew. These were not plentiful, the average age in her set being sixty-five; but there were various cousins and prep-school friends of her brother's who sometimes blew in at Mount Skellin during the annual leave from their modest employments. They were all of the squireen type, cheerful, uncouth, noticing little but what directly concerned them, concerned with little beyond the ploys of the moment.

Any of them would have expected her to drop all else the instant he appeared. Whatever it was that brought him, no matter how trivial it might be, his sheer maleness would give it priority. But Mr. Buckle saw at a glance that Sabina was tired out and Finn himself in need of refreshment. Putting his parcel aside, he took the cob from the shafts and led him to the stable, helped water and feed him, rubbed him down expertly, hissing the while like an ostler.

"I haven't done that since I was a boy," he remarked, with the sigh of an elderly man. "Now, shall I bring in the trap?"

"I'm afraid I must use it again, after Finn has rested." Sabina explained her fears for the Colonel's peace of mind. "And I can't ring him up, he's convinced that the wires are tapped."

"Then I'll run you over there myself."

"Will you really? It would be a relief! But what about you? From the look of things, you've driven some distance already."

Buckle's immaculate car had lost no time in acquiring the Inishnamona look, with the glass of one headlight broken, the fender buckled, the hood covered with scratches and speckled with the droppings of sheep.

"That was on the ferry coming home," he answered serenely. "In their haste to disembark, my fellow passengers used the car as a springboard. And I had some little ado getting off myself. The ferry sat low in the water today. But enough of that —I have something for you." And he gave the parcel he had brought into her hands with his courtly little bow.

She could hardly believe her eyes when she opened it: unaccustomed to even minor acts of consideration, she was flabbergasted by one so princely. For there were the missing taps and bung, in respect of which she had been looking forward with dread to weeks or months of negotiation! She stood turning the homely objects over and over, and when she spoke, her voice was gruff with emotion.

"Do you mean to say you drove to Dublin for them?" she growled. "Hundreds of miles, just for that?"

"I am extremely fond of motoring," was the suave reply. "And one's bath is a serious matter."

The Quiet End of Evening

There was no doubt of it, Mr. Buckle was quite unlike any male in Sabina's experience.

"Please tell me more about your Colonel," he opened up, as they set off for that gentleman's house. "People rarely get in states for no reason at all."

"You might be right," Sabina said doubtfully. She had always accepted the Colonel's mania as a fact of life, without speculation. "But I can't really think of one. One of his uncles was ambushed and shot in the Civil War. And the family house was burned down, and some of their cattle were maimed. Oh yes, and there was a story about his parents too. I believe they were locked in separate rooms for a night and each was told the other was dead. But all kinds of things went on in those days." There was a pause while she considered the question further. "It's probably something the English did," she said then, with a severe little nod. "He was in their army, you know."

"To be sure, that will be it," Mr. Buckle made haste to concur.

On reaching the Colonel's bungalow, they found his defenses improved since their call of the other day. A new and bigger lock had been fixed to the gate, while the garden wall within the palisade was freshly topped with broken glass; in the garden itself a yawning hole had been dug and covered with leafy twigs, as if for the trapping of bears. Sabina put her hand on the gate and drew it back with a startled cry.

"Aha, what d'ye think of that?" the Colonel demanded, emerging from the house. "Live wire, running to a point in the garage. Wait now, till I turn it off." Having attended to this, he hurried to let them in, plainly in high good humor. "I'm delighted you came, only sorry I've nothing to offer you. Would you believe it, the stuff isn't here yet?"

He made no allusion to the Committee's bulla, which, in fact, he had never seen. Sabina's concern, the patriots' terror, were alike unfounded, for as the paper fluttered over the wall, Snowdrop had seized and swallowed it. The new security measures were directed solely against Major Floud. Reflecting that he now had no one to talk to, the Major had decided to remit the sentence of permanent rupture, and in a stiffish note had declared himself willing to accept an apology. The Colonel had not the least idea what he meant by this; absorbed in the task of getting the sample to Dublin, on tenterhooks for Dublin's reply, he had quite forgotten the contretemps at their previous meeting, but he was damned if he would be written to in those terms, by Auberon or anyone else. If the fellow came nosing round the place looking for apologies, he would get a warm reception.

As to the euphoria of his present mood, the Colonel was bursting to share its secret. Ushering the visitors into his room, he unlocked a drawer of the desk, took from it an iron casket, unlocked that and pulled out a buff envelope adorned with a harp.

"This came today," he said. "In reply to mine. Almost by return of post. I call that efficient. Now listen," he continued reverently, as he unfolded the letter. " '*A Chara!* I am directed by the Minister of this Department to acknowledge your communication and the sample of spring water taken from your lands. The matter is under consideration and appropriate action will follow. *Mise, le meas.*' Simple, direct and to the point!" He lovingly put the letter away, locking the casket and drawer again. "My worst enemy would concede me this," he resumed with emotion. "Whenever I'm wrong, I will always admit it. In the past I have cursed those Sinn Feiners in Dublin up and down for an ignorant, lazy, corrupt set of clodhoppers and yahoos. This evening I stand here before you and take it all back. And I am glad to do so."

Sabina murmured approval of these republican sentiments, and Buckle looked earnestly at the floor.

"Well, that's enough of that," said the Colonel breezily. "Say your piece and have done is my motto. I fancy, though, things will be humming here before long. Eh, Snowdrop? Eh, Belle?" Snowdrop planted her paws on his chest and licked his ear, while Belle lay on her back and bicycled. "See that? They understand every blessed word I say. Brighter than human beings. And they don't pass it on, either. That reminds me—not a word of this to anyone but Tom, Sabby. We're not out of the wood yet."

Mr. Buckle now intervened, with suitable diffidence, to propose that they go out for a celebration, and the colonel declared it a very sound wheeze.

"But I'm afraid you'll have to pay," he added in bluff, soldierly fashion. "Things are pretty tight just now. Let's go down to Moriarty's. He's the soundest chap in the place."

"Let us do so by all means," Mr. Buckle agreed, "if Sabina likes it too."

Sabina would have liked almost anything better, but she held her peace, and as the three of them entered the lounge, flanked by Snowdrop and Belle, she was rewarded by seeing Pio turn pale and drop a bottle of Scotch.

"Butterfingers!" beamed the Colonel, wagging his head.

What did they want with him at all? Why were they there? What lay behind it? And why did they look so pleased? Such were the queries that fretted the guilt-ridden Pio as with shaking hands he poured the men their whiskey and Miss Boxham her fruit juice. The bitches were wandering about the unfamiliar room, sniffing the furniture and growling under their breath, and hoping to conceal his agitation, he passed a dry tongue over his lips and complimented the Colonel on the beautiful dogs he had. "And great company for you, Colonel, surely," he quavered. "Are they quiet? Would they go near me?"

This was a stock question in that dog-fearing neighborhood, and the Colonel was ready with his own stock reply. "Not till I told 'em," he said with a sinister chuckle.

At this Pio lost his nerve altogether. Fleeing the bar, throwing prudence to the winds, he directed his wife to take charge while he looked timorously on through a crack in the door. One of the Committee must have betrayed him, must have informed the Colonel about the vote, for he could never have made out the Irish himself, no more than any other Christian could, and there were no names to it, either. It was a shocking thing, all right, to have a Judas among you. Time was when fellows like that were found shot, dead, with a label round their neck telling why. And what class of bloody eejit was he, Moriarty, to get mixed up in it? What the divil he'd care if the Colonel insulted St. Patrick and every saint in heaven itself? It astounded him how angry he'd been when Dano came up with his foolish blether. And now it must be that the Colonel was planning some fiendish revenge; Pio had never known him so bucky. The three of them were laughing and raising their glasses and Miss Boxham was saying,

"Amen to that!" Ah, there was this in it, though, she was flying her colors at last. Wasn't that crowd all of a piece, was there one of them you could trust round the corner . . .

These somber thoughts were interrupted by cries for help. Drawing a pint of the draught for a customer in the public bar, Bernadette Moriarty had contrived to jam the lever, so that cascades of stout were drumming on the floor. It was the kind of action, impossible to anyone else, that she performed with consummate ease, and she was clamoring now for her spouse, now for the Sacred Heart, to come to the rescue. As neither responded, Buckle took the duty on himself, with the quiet efficiency that was his, while the Colonel bellowed with laughter and the bitches barked in joyous approval.

Bernadette's lamentations had roused her sleeping children, who wailed in chorus upstairs, and she thankfully hurried off to calm them, so that Pio had no choice but to leave his refuge and confront the redoubtable guests again.

"Ah, the women, the women!" he remarked with a hollow facetiousness, swabbing away at the pool of stout. "Sure, we can't turn our backs a minute! It's well for me, sir, you were there, and so handy too," he went on, addressing Mr. Buckle, who replied with some modest disclaimer. "You'll be the gentleman that's staying back at Mount Skellin, I suppose." Up to then he had been too frightened to spare a thought for this stranger, but now, hearing the English voice, he suddenly realized who it was. "You're welcome, sir, heartily welcome. We all were hearing of you."

For some days past, Mr. Buckle had in fact been a favorite topic in Moriarty's Lounge and throughout the island. Thomas might swear him to secrecy about the business they had together, and Harry Buckle might faithfully observe his vow, yet nothing much was hidden for long from the people of Inishnamona. A word dropped here, a question put there, neither of the least apparent significance, were enough; mysteriously, news seeped out and spread of itself, wafted around like thistledown on the breeze.

Pio thought fast, putting two and two together, and in his shrewd peasant fashion, making them seven or eight. After the tremendous news itself, what most engaged the local mind was the attitude of Miss Boxham to it, and the general opinion was that she must be cutting up very rough. But here she was and here was your man, wreathed in smiles and drinking away in perfect amity! It followed, then, that for the first time in his experience the general opinion was wrong. A chance offered to steer the talk into safe waters, and there seemed no harm in taking it.

"It's a grand house and a lovely property," he said. "Begod, you're the lucky man, to be getting a place like that."

No sooner were the words out than he realized his awful blunder. Miss Boxham's first reaction was one of frank interest and eager inquiry. Just what, the look she turned on Buckle seemed to say, have you been so cagily up to and why did I hear nothing of it before? That look vanished at once as the truth of the matter came home. Pio could only refer to Mount Skellin, for no other local property warranted his description. She paused, breathless, waiting for Mr. Buckle to refute the absurd suggestion, but he, poised and imperturbable, was coloring up and staring into his glass with a foolish grin, like any convicted schoolboy. Now the color left her face and her heart was ready to burst with rage; she felt as if it were in her mouth and she would suffocate. The enormity was such that she could not grasp it all at a blow. The dastardly part that Thomas had played would have to be gone into later. At this moment the villain was Buckle, that false and scheming Saxon, artfully winning her golden opinions, slyly canvassing her good graces, lulling her just suspicions to sleep while he perfected his fiendish plans. For a long minute she glared at him as he mumbled and fidgeted with his glass; then, in a voice low and vibrant with passion, she pronounced the single word "Grabber!" and, tempestuously, swept from the Up-To-Date Lounge into the quiet, starry night.

"Did Miss Boxham not know then, sir?" Pio inquired, abashed but curious as ever. "She seemed a little put out."

"No, we didn't tell her," Mr. Buckle said ruefully. "Her brother wished it to be between us until everything was fixed. May I ask how you came to hear?"

"I suppose it was mentioned here in the bar," said Pio, suddenly vague. "My own idea is, everyone knew, except for the lady. Sure, there's nothing to do in this country, only mind other men's business." His eye returned to its normal acuteness. "A place like Mount Skellin—I daresay it would fetch a good round figure?"

"I daresay you are right," Mr. Buckle responded.

Busy with his thoughts, the Colonel had taken in nothing of all this.

"Sabby gone home, has she now?" he inquired. "On foot? Six miles if it's a step. That's a fine girl. Pity she wasn't a boy. She'd have had the place and made it pay, fruit, honey, eggs, that kind of thing. There's never any fruit round here. Months since I tasted an apple. Thomas does nothing but lie about. Sabby's the better fellow. Has the makings of a soldier, too, good Gurkha material. Would have had, I mean. Rather silly thing to say, really. It's the drink, I'm not used to it. Better get home, if you'll kindly give me a lift. Not a word, remember, about that letter from Dublin. You can't trust any of the natives here, they're like Burmese. Except for Moriarty," he bestirred himself to remark drowsily as the car started off. "His father was in the Connaught Rangers."

Ten

THE FIRST THOUGHT of Thomas Boxham, on hearing Buckle's report, was for himself and his own immunity. He at once secured the outer doors and ground-floor windows and lifted the telephone receiver from its rest; and after that he packed his luggage in readiness for an early departure the following day. Only when these preparations were completed did he give his mind to the case as such.

"I can't even surmise how our plans leaked out," he declared. "Eavesdropping would be on the cards, of course, but as far as I remember we only talked about this in the open, away from the bushes, or when the staff had gone home for the night. I really sometimes think old Sentence is not so cracky at all. Our houses may be bugged."

"I shall go to England," he replied to a question from Harry. "As I intended doing, once the affair was settled. This makes no difference to our arrangement. I insist on your remaining a full month at least before you decide—longer if you wish. If then you still want to take on this nightmare, it's yours."

"There is no if about it," Harry assured him.

Thomas heaved a weary sigh. "What is it in Ireland that makes even the brightest English silly?" he demanded. "Which of the Irish lines have you swallowed? The spiritual enclave in the desert of crass materialism? Let me translate: it only means that their indolence, on the whole, is greater than their greed."

"Well, there is nothing like a change," Harry observed. "It was the other way round in London. With my colleagues, that is; with my labor force, the two things were about evenly matched."

The ferry sat lower still in the water the next day as Harry brought his friend to the Dublin train, and he thought it seemed lower again on his return to Inishnamona.

"I fancy you'll change your tune before long," Thomas had said, in taking leave. "Remember, you are not committed. You are free as the air. Which is rather good of me, considering how I ache for freedom myself." He had a last word of warning. "Don't delude yourself that Sabby will come round—she won't."

Sabina had been on Harry's mind all through the evening before and in wakeful spells during the night. His first reaction to the epithet she hurled at him was one of guilt, of a feeling it must somehow be deserved. He did not know what a grabber was in the Irish sense; far less did he realize that she merely used the term as an expletive, chosen at random from a set of other emotive terms, in relief to herself rather than definition of him. His understanding of the charge was that without scruple or delicacy, he had jumped at, snatched up, a bargain offered lightly and without due heed by its present owner, and his immediate impulse was to give up the whole idea. With this in mind, after leaving the Colonel at Simla, he had driven in haste down the road to her village, expecting to overtake her, to explain, apologize and be forgiven.

The plan was foiled, however, by Sabina herself. Seeing his lights and hearing his engine, she hid behind a rock until the car had passed. And as time went by, the second thoughts came too: he could not find his conduct so reprehensible. Mount Skellin belonged to a man as eager to sell as he was to buy—how, when all was said and done, did Sabina come into the picture at all? She was very much at home in the place, always in and out, but there was no reason for change in that respect. If he were to back out now, and Thomas sold to a stranger, the doors would be shut for good. Presently he began to think that he was doing Miss Boxham a favor.

And the place had captivated him from the moment he set eyes upon it. With its voices that murmured of things gone by and its air of slipping through life in a perpetual dream, it was the antithesis of everything he loathed and was fleeing. All that would have marked it down in the view of normal buyers constituted for him the chief attractions: size, waste, neglect, abandon and decay. He was sick of things that functioned smoothly and to no real purpose; in his alienation from them he, the dandified and punctilious, was at one with the mop-headed, grubby protesters and opters-out. It meant nothing to him that in the few years since he took on the family business it had doubled in scope. Pop men, younger than he, made far greater piles by simply bawling and gibbering. The business itself, cause of triumphant elation in the board room, struck him as a classic example of decline. In the eighteenth century young Richard Buckle, of laboring stock, had blossomed out as a designer and carver of beautiful furniture, a Buckle chair, bed or desk being appreciated to this day, and the firm started by him had flourished ever since, surviving, growing, and after the industrial revolution, cheerfully adapting to lower standards and inferior tastes. Harry's contribution had been to invent and promote a number of lines suitable to the cramped environments of the day; a bookcase that turned into a bed at night, the books being left undisturbed, was commonly reckoned his masterpiece. There was no knowing what other marvels of compression he might, with time, have engendered, but on his twenty-seventh birthday he had announced to the horrified board his intention of retiring at once. Deaf to argument or appeal, he had sold out and joyfully prepared to take a long, long rest. An old invitation from the friend of his Oxford days, Thomas Boxham, came to mind and he wrote a careful letter; by return, a time- and trouble-saving wire begged him to consider Mount Skellin his own, and within a very few hours of arriving there, he found that this might literally come to pass.

He was now sitting at breakfast, for which there had been no time before the drive to the station, and considering how to spend his day. That was a luxury in itself: here, nothing was fixed, immovably arranged, the hours were not laid out in advance for this or that purpose but flowed peacefully by, one after the other, without his marking them. He was not proposing to be idle, but he would do only the things he enjoyed, and the future smiled so sweetly at him that he could scarcely believe in it.

Suddenly the door flew open and a stranger bounced in, with a jovial cry of "Ah, young slugabed, here you are!" Then, pulling himself up, he said, "I beg your pardon. I am looking for Boxham."

Harry rose to his feet and wished him good morning. "I am afraid that Thomas has gone to Dublin," he said politely.

The newcomer stared at him, taken aback. He was tall and thin, with an egg-shaped head, the bald crown rising from a fringe of silvery hair, a monkeyish face and small, suspicious, dark eyes. "To Dublin? Impossible. He never goes anywhere," he retorted with a certain impatience.

"I have just driven him to the station," Harry assured him.

"But look here, I telephoned last night and he asked me to come round this morning," the man persisted. "By the way, I'm Floud, Major Floud. Who are you?"

Harry introduced himself and explained that circumstances had arisen which caused a change of plans. "Our telephone doesn't function after nine at night or before nine in the morning," he said, "or I feel sure he would have let you know."

"Yes, yes, the telephone, damn nuisance, but did he say nothing? Left no word with you?"

Harry was obliged to admit there was none. "I am so sorry about it," he said. "Is there anything I can do?"

"You? No." Major Floud seemed not to care for the looks of Mr. Buckle. "This is a rum go, to be sure," he remarked severely. "I saw a woman out in the yard and asked where the master might be. She told me in here, having his breakfast. Then I find you, by yourself, and the table set for one." He glared round the room as if expecting to find Thomas, gagged and bound, in a corner. "But you tell me you drove him to Ballycagey to catch the train."

"And so I did," Harry confirmed in a rather absent tone. His mind was busy with the fact of Bridie or Maggie regarding him now as the master; he had not, as yet, traveled so far himself.

"Is that your car in the drive?" the Major pursued, with the air of a man determined to come at the truth.

"I imagine so. Mine is a white Volvo."

"It looks as if you were in a smash. Both headlights gone."

"That was on the ferry," was the placid explanation. "One went yesterday, the other today."

"You seem to move about a great deal," the Major observed resentfully. "When does Boxham get back?"

"That is something I can't tell you, but I think not for a while," Mr. Buckle answered with a wistful look at his bacon and eggs. "He is going on to England."

"To England!" repeated the Major, aghast. "Whereabouts in England?"

"I don't know that either, but I suppose it may be London."

"He has left no address?"

"None."

"But this is absurd! This is preposterous!" the Major argued. "I have an appointment with Boxham here. The servant says he is in and at breakfast. You say he has gone to England, you don't know where, why or for how long. There is something fishy about it. Fishy."

Mr. Buckle was growing tired of the Major. "I am sorry you should think so," he said suavely, sitting down and resuming his meal. "I have told you all I know and can do no more."

His interrogator was not to be fobbed off easily. "May I venture to ask what you are doing here yourself?" he inquired with a searching look at the victim, up and down, as if his pockets bulged with the Boxham silver; but he had gone too far.

"I am here by invitation, oddly enough," Buckle stated. "Now, if you are sure I can do nothing to help, perhaps I ought not to detain you."

At the ring of steel in the gentle voice, the Major hauled down his colors. "No offense, my boy," he said lamely. "Fact is, I want to speak to Thomas on a matter of great importance, and it upset me to find him gone. So unlike him, don't you know, he hardly stirs from the house."

Despondently he took his leave. It was untrue that he had anything of importance to say to Thomas. He had intended breaking the news of the Colonel's being a poisoner, but that was peripheral; what he really looked for was company. The whole morning could have been whiled away and Thomas would have asked him to luncheon. Since the breach with Sentence he had come to see how blank his life was and how limited his resource. Apart from rereading Dornford Yates, he had done nothing of any interest. Twice he had called in the doctor on some pretext, but that overworked gentleman merely glanced at him, declared that his health was a bloody marvel and rushed away. Mrs. Tooth had not returned from Rapallo; he did not hold with the new Rector, whom he always referred to as Johnny Jump-Up; and he had fallen out with nearly everyone else. But Thomas was always at home, always pleasant, and being too idle to talk himself, always ready to listen.

It was disappointment, then, more than real suspicion that

led to the heckling of Mr. Buckle, but now something occurred to call up suspicion in earnest. Sweeping the hall was a woman whom the Major took for the one who had misdirected him. Not only were the features identical, but she too wore a flowered apron over a black serge dress, stout boots laced to the calf, thick white woollen stockings and a kerchief printed with scenes from Killarney. The Major had often heard of the twins and seen them about together, but he lacked retention: unless a thing directly concerned him, he forgot it at once. He bore down upon the culprit and opened the prosecution.

"Why did you tell me Mr. Thomas was in the dining room?" he demanded. "You must have known it wasn't true."

"Indeed then, I told you no such thing," the woman said with a toss of the head. "I never saw you at all."

This blatant falsehood fairly took the Major's breath away. "Come now, think what you're saying," he adjured her. "It was just a few minutes ago, out in the yard."

Bridie or Maggie was not going to enlighten the man, with his loud voice and ignorant manner. Both resented the eternal confusing of one with the other, a slight family resemblance being all they would own to; for, devoted as they were, each considered herself far and away the more attractive of the two. "I wasn't there," she said, going on with her work. "I didn't go out since I got here at nine. Anyway, I wouldn't have said it about Mr. Thomas, for I haven't an idea in the world where he is."

"You are not speaking the truth," rasped the Major.

"Is it call me a liar?" cried the woman. "I didn't see Mr. Thomas since yesterday evening, and he at his supper. There's one thing I'll tell you, though," she proceeded, as her imagination caught fire, "he never slept in his bed last night!"

"Then the fellow in there, the stranger—he didn't drive to the station this morning at all?" the Major exclaimed.

"Divil a bit of it," his informant replied. "He only came down the stairs, sedate as a bishop, and said to cook breakfast for one."

"Then where can the master be? What has become of him?"

"That's something the man in there could maybe tell us," Maggie or Bridie whispered with a meaningful glance at the dining-room door.

In a minute or so the Major was off to Sabina, buoyed up by the prospect of trouble and a happy new sense of importance, while the twins rocked with laughter over a cup of tea.

Having finished his breakfast in peace, Harry set out on a leisurely tour of the demesne. With the house itself he was already familiar, for Thomas had seen to that; indeed, there was something sublime in the way that he, longing to discard it, had exposed its every defect and blemish. The various stairs that were taller or shorter than the rest, so that running down you could easily trip and break your neck; the windows that could not be opened, for fear of their tumbling out altogether; floorboards unsafe as thawing ice; the likelihood that before very long part of the roof would fall in; and the certainty that if fire broke out the whole place would burn to the ground before help could arrive, and yourself with it if you happened to be in one of the towers—all these matters, and the impossibility of ever finding people to set them right, had been scrupulously brought to the young man's attention.

And the house had seemed to respond to the generosity of

its owner, discovering a range of resource new even to him. He was well used to a stream of earwigs when he turned on a bath tap, but to these were now added twigs, leaves and feathers, which he identified as from the rookery, although quite at a loss to determine how they entered the system. The family portraits began falling to earth like so many ripe plums. More spectacular still, the septic tank overflowed: walking up the drive, the two young men had found an inexplicable wave rushing down it toward them, and ever since then the plumbing had moaned and gurgled like a fiend in torment.

"Who knows what it may not think of next?" said Thomas, to whom the place was a living being, sentient and malign. "There's nothing I'd put beyond it." But these and other capers only attached Mr. Buckle the more.

For the lands, however, he had feelings of another sort. He was going to bring them back into kindness. He would restore the shrubberies, rid the orchards of disease, revive the fruit and vegetable gardens, return the lawns to their ancient beauty, clear and stock the streams, plant flowers everywhere. There should be lambs, chickens, calves, piglets, wandering freely in sun or rain under the sky, not gasping out their lives in cells and catacombs. It was something of a program, perhaps, but he was quite resolved to carry it through.

He wandered out to the terrace and stood awhile, drinking the prospect in. The weather held, the sun poured down, the sea twinkled and shimmered, in the sky there was hardly a cloud. It would of course not be always so. There were gales to come, and stinging rain, angry white-crested waves, falling trees, floods, but for the moment it seemed like heaven itself. At the sight of his maltreated car, he chuckled aloud. The to-do in London if some-body's paint got a scratch! Here, nothing of that sort mattered at all. He felt blissfully reborn into another world of broader and kinder dimensions, infinitely rich and promising all the heart could desire.

A stout, ungainly bird settled on the telegraph wire over his head, followed by another and then another.

Cuckoo! came the raucous aggressive cry. Cuckoo! Cuckoo!

For some time they kept this up, then suddenly changed as one to their other call, a throaty clucking and burping, like old men laughing feebly together, and clumsily flew away.

Eleven

SABINA WAS LOOKING peaked and wan, after a miserable night. The long walk home in darkness after the many fatigues of the day had exhausted her; too weary to sleep, she lay tossing and turning and thinking of Buckle. She of course knew nothing of his reasons, of the circumstances in his own past life that drove him on to his present behavior. It never struck her that he probably had no idea of what the place meant to herself. The services he had rendered, partly from kindliness, partly in the innocent hope of winning her favor, now appeared as maneuvers, base and abominable; even the bath taps had become symbols of English perfidy. As soon as the sun rose she was up, intending to drive to Mount Skellin and harangue, cajole or threaten her brother until he came to his senses. But Finn was wheezing and limping from the exertions of the day before, and could not be expected to work. She was too tired to make the journey on foot, and so she sat at home, grieving and brooding, until roused by the unwelcome sight of Major Floud tripping down her garden path.

He had never been a favorite of hers, and his hollow, old-man's voice jarred more than usual today; nor was she in the mood for senile fantasies and foreshadowings of doom. Nothing surprised her less, she told him, coolly and incisively, than that Thomas should have decamped. On grounds which she need not disclose, it was the most natural thing in the world. When the Major persisted, she wearily picked up the telephone and put in a call to the stationmaster, who confirmed that Mr. Boxham had caught the morning train.

"Say what you like," argued the Major, whose beliefs were seldom shaken by evidence. "The woman told me he was at breakfast. Then she denied having said it at all. She also assured me he hadn't slept in his bed, and broadly hinted that the fellow staying there was up to some mischief."

"That part of it may well be true," Sabina said grimly. "But you can ignore the rest. Buckle would have returned from Bally-cagey before the women arrived for work, and they never reach the bedrooms until the afternoon. She was putting you on—it's what they all do."

The Major had lived there for a quarter century without noting this regional habit. "I venture to disagree," he replied stiffly. "I flatter myself, I know when people are telling the truth. That was a badly frightened woman. Mark my words, something is up."

Muttering, he took himself off to bring this view to wider notice. The island, ever prone to believe the worst, no matter how shaky the source, heard him with pleasure and hastened to fill in the blanks for itself. Missing, Mr. Thomas undoubtedly was; and even those who had actually witnessed his departure joined in the speculation as to where he might now be: down a bog hole or over the cliff, at the bottom of the pool or immured in his own cellar. All of them, in retrospection, clearly recalled mistrusting the English fellow the instant they clapped eyes on him.

As the Major drove off, Twomey's van drew up at the gate and Dr. Plummie, the Protestant Bishop, climbed out. As often when he visited this parish, there was an aggrieved look on his broad red face. The parish consisted of thirteen souls and it gave him more trouble than all the others combined. The previous Rector had been an affable dotard who never raised a finger, and in his day there was absolute peace. But after his death the Bishop installed what he described as a live wire, although there was nothing in the parish on which the live wire could usefully play. As a result, nearly everyone was at loggerheads, united only in dislike of their pastor. Whenever the Bishop looked in, there seemed to be some new bone of contention. The Colonel and the Major refused to worship unless "God Save the Queen" were sung and various regimental flags displayed. Mrs. Prout was trying to oust Mrs. Dove from her function as organist: Mrs. Dove threatened, and was fully prepared, sooner to blow up the harmonium. There had been a bout of fisticuffs between Mr. Craig and Dr. Ballantyne over a plot in the churchyard, where both particularly wished to be buried.

The Bishop marched down the path and into the house without formality. "Here's a nice thing, Sabina," he said, throwing himself into a chair. "Tom was to see me this morning and he's hoofed it. We were to discuss repairs to the church—I mean, of course, I was looking for a check. An awful time I had of it, too, getting over. Wasn't going to risk the car on that ferry. One of the fishermen rowed me across." And indeed his hat, gaiters and apron were studded with pearly scales.

Sabina was delighted to see him. People often were, when their problems were of a secular kind. His was a late vocation, so late in the opinion of some as not yet to have made an appearance, and he had started life in the law. Thomas' conduct was so outrageous that Sabina thought it must be illegal. There would have to be, in her view, machinery to prevent such doings if human society were not to be a fraud and a sham, but the Bishop, after listening attentively to the indictment, soon dashed this hope.

"I'm afraid you haven't a leg," he told her bluntly. "In France, now, as presumptive heir you might have a say. But there's nothing here to stop a man doing as he likes with his own. Who's the buyer—the charming young fellow I spoke to?"

"That's not how I should describe him," Sabina said.

"Come now, that's prejudice. Natural enough, but leads nowhere. I'm sorry to disappoint you," he added, for she looked as sad as a child robbed of its toy. "Now, if Thomas turned Catholic, we might dispossess him and get him hanged into the bargain," the Bishop continued in a lighter vein; he was a mine of curious information. "There's an old statute to that effect, left on the book and never repealed. But he'd have to turn first, and it might be dicey at that, you know."

He burst into a merry laugh, but even the thought of Thomas hanged could not coax a smile from his sister.

"There must be something I can do, there must!" she cried,

unable, like the resolute woman she was, to accept the idea of impotence.

"I don't know what, except make the best of things. And I really can't blame old Tom. Wish I could be rid of the palace! Forty rooms, and all as damp as washing day. Big houses belong to the past. Last week I saw an advert in the Ballycagey *Bugle:* 'For Sale—fine old Georgian residence, suitable for demolition.' And that's about the size of it."

"Father used to talk like that, but he never dreamed of selling," Sabina retorted bitterly. "Tom's a renegade and a traitor. And he's anti-Irish. And an idle good-for-nothing. And a coward as well, running off like that, rather than face me."

"We're none of us perfect," Dr. Plummie observed. "And men are often scared of sisters." He placed the tips of his fingers together and ruminated a little in silence; then a mighty grin split his face, pushing his cheeks up to his eyes. "I say, look here!" he cried. "I've had a marvelous wheeze. Why don't you marry the young Englishman? That would turn the tables on Master Tom and no mistake."

"Not if he were the last man alive!" Sabina exploded.

"That's morbid," said her ghostly counselor, unmoved. "Just you take my advice and collar him. You'll bring it off nicely. I've always thought it would be best if you married money. It's always best if people can. And then you'll move into the ancestral hall and Tom can be asked to stay at Christmas."

With that, he bethought himself of Twomey's patiently waiting van and took his leave. "I hope the new boy's a church-goer," were his parting words. "He might come down with something substantial."

Once he had gone, Sabina felt more despondent than ever. It was not merely the Bishop's failure to come up with an apropos point of law that distressed her, but his deplorable point of view. She had expected sympathy and understanding at least; all she got was facetious comment and tasteless advice. Her face burned anew at the recollection. Dr. Plummie spoke of marriage in the cold-blooded way of the people, who would urge a son to unite himself with the girl next door and secure her farm: he had the mind of a peasant, for all his gaiters and hat. Still worse, he had taken her brother's side, and if he did so, everyone else would do it too: there would be no support for her claims or concern for her deprivation. But she was not the woman to collapse without a struggle and soon she was hard at work, devising campaigns by the dozen.

Elsewhere on the island, things were going forward too. The Colonel had got up with the lark as usual that morning and had driven his cow from Mick Slattery's field to one belonging to Mrs. Tooth a couple of miles away. This was done, like most of his deeds, to give himself the illusion of employment, but when Mick left his own bed, hours later, and found the animal gone, he assumed the Committee's action to be the cause and hurried off to apprise the Chairman. The two of them were still anxiously pondering it, surmising who could have done the translation, or fearing, God help us, that the Colonel had the Irish after all, asking themselves if his driving the cow was to be taken as a portent of good or an omen of harm, when the postman hove into the lounge with a letter bearing the escutcheon, familiar to all in those parts, of Bord Failte.

What the Board had to say depressed them further. The gist

of it was that no definite reply could be given without a great deal more information as to why a grant was requested and how it was going to be spent; but on the face of things it appeared as if the pageant would come within the scope of the Arts Council rather than of themselves, a tourist promotion body.

The entire communication breathed a spirit of damping indifference.

"Is it anything strange if men leave the country?" the Chairman asked with pathos. "Why do we want a grant! Sure, any fool would know that. And if you don't mind, how's it going to be spent! That is our own business entirely."

"They're getting awful sticky, that crowd," Micky Malone complained. "And the rest of them too, with the dole and the pension and all. You'd think the money came out of their pockets. Did you hear about Barney Roche?"

Barney Roche was the pride of Inishnamona. He could spot a mushroom growing a hundred yards away; he could detect a fox that, wraithlike, slid through bracken tawny as itself; he could place seven darts out of eight in the bull's-eye, *tac tac tac*. It was not for these gifts, however, that he was reverenced, admirable though they were. What raised him to a pinnacle was that for upward for thirteen years, he had been drawing the blind man's pension. In local eyes, he stood for the ideal, for what was soaring and free, differentiating man from brute: he was the island's soul, it might be said, as Jeanne d'Arc was the soul of France.

Hearing that name, Pio pricked up his ears at once. "No, what?" he demanded, staring. "I saw him at confession Saturday, but we didn't get talking."

Micky glanced cautiously around and sank his voice to a

whisper. "They were saying how he's to be investigated!"

Pio shuddered with horror and indignation. "If they'd do that, they'd do anything," he cried passionately. "There's hardly worse in Russia."

"What do they balk at, these days? Didn't they stop Paddy Flaherty's dole, the decent man?" Micky continued the indictment. "Only for he'd won the poor little coupla thousand, out of the Sweep?"

"Ah, the whole bloody place is gone rotten."

"You know what I think, Pio? It's a case of victimization. On account of our proclaiming the island."

"More than likely. That's Dublin for you! The British were never as bad."

For a while they gave themselves up to the pleasure of cursing the Government. Then, turning to practical issues, they debated how Bord Failte might be woo'd and won. So eagerly had their minds fastened on the hope of a grant that at the very suggestion it might be refused, they felt actually out of pocket. The Chairman thought to bring the grandeur of the project home by forwarding Rowty's script, and urgent word was sent to the author to furnish a copy, but here was an unlooked-for snag in that he had put nothing so far on paper. He willingly left his work, however, to come and reassure them. It was due to no lack of ideas, quite the reverse. Fresh scenes and new images kept crowding his brain, so brilliant and vivid and fancy that to reduce them to little black marks on a heap of paper seemed in the nature of anticlimax. He spoke so well, this man of the people, wearing the plain white coat of his trade, waxed so eloquent, with such a loftiness of intonation, as to carry his hearers with him; it was only after he had gone, and Micky too, that Pio fell a prey to doubt.

It was on the cards, he mused, that the whole idea would come to nothing. All the Committee's other ideas had done so, in a way that seemed extraordinary. By now the pattern was well established. First, someone came up with a brilliant scheme which fired every brain, the carpings of that chronic caviller Niall McCarthy merely acting as a bellows. The schemes varied in nature but were all magnificent, grandiose even, in concept. There was to have been a regatta, quite putting Cowes in the shade. There was to have been the Olympic games, after which the athletes would vote to hold all subsequent meetings here. There was to have been a horse show, to the despair of the Royal Dublin Society and its total eclipse. The members' ardent imagination visualized these triumphs in glowing detail, their boundless faith in themselves would allow nothing to be beyond their reach; but when they tried to make the arrangements it all collapsed like a bubble.

Was the life of Patrick, Apostle of Ireland, to be yet another fiasco? Would Oberammergau continue unchallenged? Could Inishnamona fail where thick German peasants succeeded? To know oneself the superior, yet to see oneself forever surpassed— could anguish be keener? Yet for all their qualities of wit and poetic genius, what had they done, so far, toward that radiant luminous vision of their island's destiny?

To this last question, at any rate, Pio could give the reply. They had made right fools of themselves, listening to Dano's blether; in all probability they had piqued the Colonel, who never forgot, and they had undoubtedly annoyed Miss Boxham.

That was the sum of their achievement, and it was in the old tradition.

If only he could sell the pub or if only his wife were still as she was when they married, cute as a fox and able for anyone, he'd clear off to England. But his wife was a spent force, and who was going to buy a pub round here, with trade slackening off all the time? Pio could no longer conceal from himself the truth about that blowing up. It had been glorious all right, for the moment, bringing the parties concerned a satisfaction they had never known before: an undertaking of theirs, at last, in every sense, had got off the ground. But now reality was here, in the bar, his sole custom the regular crowd with their dreary familiar faces, their jokes and feuds and stories so often told, the sap was all dried out. And even the regulars dropped away in lovely weather like this, going to Mahony's below, where they had tables outside and parasols over them and every old frenchified gimmick.

This melancholy train of thought was shattered by the youngest boy, an apple-cheeked rascal of nine, who burst in demanding a Coca-Cola. It was a settled thing that he had one every day on returning from school, but all he got now was a cuff on the ear and the advice to be off. Filled with a sense of wrong, he opened a cavernous mouth and began to yell, his normal method of persuasion, and was promptly cuffed again.

"Bernadette, will you come here and get the lad out of it!" his father bawled, his nerves ajangle. "How'm I supposed to think me thoughts with the shindy that's going on?"

His wife trudged in, weary and hot, with a broom in her hand. "He only wants his Coke," she roared in successful competition with her progeny. "I said he could get it."

"Did you, well! And I'm after saying he couldn't," Pio shouted, banging his fist on the bar in a kind of frenzy. "I'm not giving away any Cokes, not if 'twas God Himself and His Mother that asked for them!"

"The Lord save us!" muttered the startled wife, for she had never known him to use such talk; as a rule his references to the powers above were circumspect and promotional. "Go on now, Michael, and don't be plaguing your da," she commanded, pushing the broomstick into the boy's chubby paw. "Take the broom, there's the great man, and go beat the dog."

Sniveling, Michael took the broom and left the bar, and a piteous yelping arose outside.

"He'll enjoy that, now, better than any Coke," said the landlord, calming down. "But don't send the kids in again looking for drink, you hear me. The rate we're going, I'll be out of business be the New Year. If the end of the world doesn't come first."

Which might, he reflected, be the handiest solution, at that.

Twelve

It MAY BE darkest before the dawn, but equally, when things appear to be looking up, catastrophe is often just round the corner. At this particular moment two events gave a fillip to the island morale, awaking a spirit of optimism that was all the keener for being wholly unfounded.

The first and lesser of these was the investigation of Barney Roche by the Pensions man from Ballycagey. A local fellow nominally carried out these duties and actually drew a salary for them, but he had better sense than to report on neighbors adversely, so that cases like this were always reviewed from outside.

It was typical of the mean, crabbed un-Irish way the department conducted its affairs that no word of the pending visit was given to Barney himself. Even the Guards, whose etiquette these days left much to be desired, never raided an honest man out of the blue without giving him a chance to hide the still or close the bar or take whatever avoiding action was called for, but Pensions loved to work by stealth and surprise. Thanks to the island intelligence service, it was known that something of the kind was on the cards, but the details were a closely kept secret; and on the evening of the pounce Barney was up on his roof, pointing the slates and enjoying the sun, without a care in the world.

He spotted the fellow a long way off, noting that he was alien, surmising that he was up to no good, but not immediately rumbling his intention. The man wore a city slicker's hat on his head, while Inishnamona wore berets or bonnets; he had a good tweed suit instead of jeans and sweater; and he marched over the ground in a purposeful way, whereas islanders strolled along as if they had no real object in moving. He had "local government" written all over him and was surely there to stick his nose in some poor bugger's business. But now he stopped on the road to speak to a child, who turned in Barney's direction, pointing toward his house; and then, after patting her cheek like a candidate for the Dáil, he strode forward again, brisker than ever.

A stranger asking for him meant only one thing. Barney was down the ladder and into the kitchen with the speed of light, calling for Mary, his wife. By the time the visitor reached the door, the pair of them offered a moving example of affliction bravely borne and compassionate service to it. Barney sat by the window, his poor sightless eyes shielded from the glare of the sun by dark spectacles, while Mary read aloud from the *Bugle*. There was infinite pathos in the way he turned his head toward the newcomer, asking in the diffident, hesitant manner of the blind, "What is it, Mary *alanna?* Who wants us, my dear?" as, groping for the white walking stick at his elbow, he knocked it to the floor. "Ah, God love him, the decent man!" cried Mary on cue as she ran to pick it up and place it in his fumbling hand.

The interview went quite differently from what the officer had envisaged. He had resolved to demand a certificate from the Ballycagey eye man, and had sunk so low as to think of little dodges for tripping Barney up. The anonymous informant had stated, with a wealth of supporting detail, that he had the eyes of a gull, but in the presence of this suffering man, this tenderly devoted woman, the allegations seemed to melt away, like mist in the morning sun. The inspector was a young man, new to the district, and the official records were of no help to him. They were as tantalizingly episodic as the trailer of a film. Nothing was said in them of how long Barney had been on the pension, nor of how he came to be there, but there was a confidential note revealing that his father had thrice been jailed for Ireland. All things weighed together, the prudent course was to assure Mr. Roche of the visit being simple routine, and after a little friendly chat, to go away, and this the officer did.

It was a characteristic of Inishnamona that when faced with external threat all private cares were put away, and men, women and children worked selflessly together as one. No sooner had the news flashed round of a city fellow asking for Barney than arrangements were put in hand. The departing inspector found that the ferry had moved to the opposite shore, the ferry master having, bystanders said, gone to a christening on the mainland. By happy chance a fisherman was there, mending his net, and volunteered to row him back for a trifle of four pounds. After discussion lasting an hour, this was reduced by three shillings and sixpence, and the inspector gingerly took his seat in the curragh, which danced about as curraghs will, to his trepidation, while every stroke of the oar drenched him with spray. The crowning touch, however, was one for which the glory belonged to God alone: when the curragh was halfway across, a fresh evening breeze sprang up and the intruder's hat sailed off on the tide.

The rout of the government forces filled every heart with jubilation. Just as the hunger, tedium and peril of wartime is forgotten in joy at a victory, so Barney's triumph dispelled for a time the gloomy doubts and fears that weighed on the local mind. A man of education, well dressed, well paid, in authority and with a fancy class of accent, had pitted his wits against those of an Inishnamona man and got himself nicely beat, and if Barney could do it, so might they all, and prove a match for the world.

The second occurrence made even greater impact, being shrouded in mystery and thus leaving a wider scope for the imagination. Two more strangers appeared, of the same city cut, and installed themselves in the leading hotel. What their business was the proprietor, for all his skilled inquiry, could not discover; but business they undoubtedly had, as proved by their luggage, which included a typewriter, briefcases, files, and a number of instruments such as no one had ever seen before.

This paraphernalia was kept under lock and key when not in use, that is to say, for practically the entire time. Shortly after the strangers arrived, they were seen to call on Colonel Sentence, taking their gear along, and to spend a morning prowling about

his land and the hillside above. From this expedition they returned in a curious frame of mind, talking very fast, but in low
voices, and with frequent bursts of laughter. They remained on
the island awhile, exploring, boating, trout fishing, playing poker
and drinking in the bars, always in a sunny, carefree mood, yet
always watchful and quick to parry attempts to draw them out.
Then one evening the pair of them sat down, and with gales of
merriment, composed a document on a long sheet of official paper, and in the morning they were gone.

The keenest of brains were puzzled to account for it all.
The one man apparently in the know was Colonel Sentence,
an application to whom, did anyone dare to make it, would
simply be a waste of time. For once, the strangers having
written and received no letters and made no use of the telephone, Delia, the postmistress and telephone operator, was
unable to help. There was little indeed to work on, and that
little open to various interpretation, but the people went
about it with a will and hardly talked of anything else. Some
thought the strangers intended to shoot a colossal epic film,
costing millions and employing the entire population; others,
that they were looking for a site on which to build a mammoth hotel; others again, that they were on the track of a vast
hoard of gold, buried for centuries in the bog. All were
agreed, however, that fellows who spent their money so freely
and had so much time on their hands must be in a very big
way, and that whatever they might be up to, the prospects for
Inishnamona were rosy.

These were but dreams, but the realm of dreams was their

motherland, in which they felt at home and able to function. They were as cheered and comforted by the fruits of their fancy as if these had a solid existence outside it. But now something occurred on the cruel material plane where they never quite found their bearings, always were helpless and lost. In the full light of day—slowly, calmly, as it were deliberately—the ferryboat sank.

With it, the last of its kind in Irish waters, went all hope of supplies other than what could be rowed across in skiff or curragh. Inishnamona saw itself reduced to the primitive level of those few outer islands that still supported life. No tourists now need come, for they could not be entertained. Even the monthly fair, at which people sold their calves and lambs to dealers from inland, would have to stop, for who would venture back in a small boat with struggling, kicking beasts aboard? Every car on the island would be laid by; food would be short, and duller if possible than now; and the very pubs might have to close, when every spark of animation would disappear.

The euphoria of recent days vanished in a trice and was followed by a mood of dark suspicion. As the island modes of thought demanded, all refused to believe that the ferry had sunk from mere decrepitude. News of hidden matters might travel here with supernatural speed, as if, volatilized, it floated on the breeze to solidify in some expectant ear; but let any event take place in the sight of all, for reasons clearly sufficient, and it was never allowed to be as simple as it appeared. Much else must always lie behind it, and in the case of disaster, someone not themselves be found to blame. For a long time now, the old ferry had wheezed and groaned and rattled more painfully, moved more awkwardly, sat deeper in the water, but in spite of this the people suspected sabotage. An enemy had done it, from what motives they could not at once determine, but all resolved to find him out, and when they had done so, to execute upon him a vengeance swift and terrible.

Thirteen

ABSOLUTE CALM HAD REIGNED as the ferry went down. There was no panic, no scrambling to be ahead, no unseemly conduct of the kind that too often attends marine disaster. For this laudable state of affairs, an explanation offered. Apart from Dermot, the ferry master, who knew how shallow the sea was there, the only person making the trip was Mrs. Tooth, back from her winter in Rapallo. She was a vague, placid woman, seldom alive to her surroundings, and she noticed nothing until the water was up to her knees and sundry pieces of lighter baggage were bobbing about on the surface. Then she scrambled onto the roof, where, as soon as the ferry struck bottom, the master joined her, and the two of them sat there in safety and comfort until a boat put out and took them off.

It was a strange homecoming altogether. Mrs. Tooth had written in plenty of time to Major Floud asking him kindly to meet her train; but the General Post Office, for the second time that year, was working to rule and the letter still reposed in Dublin. The merry, handsome young porter, who always hailed her return with such delight, was gone to England, replaced by an elderly gnome with arthritis. After an hour in the waiting room, with nothing to amuse her but the self-laudatory advertisements of Córeas Iompair Eireann, she telephoned to the Major, only to hear that she had not been expected. The Major further tried to explain about their new island status, which had come into being since she left in the autumn before; but his words were drowned by a curious bubbling on the line which often thwarted communication in this area. When at last by various makeshifts she got herself to the sound, the wreck of their natural causeway came as a total surprise. Unruffled and uncomplaining, she had embarked on the ferry, with the result described; and she was rewarded at last, on reaching land, by the sight of the Major hurrying to greet her.

"Rosemary, my dear! How good to see you." And he kissed her warmly on either cheek, still peachy and pink in her sixty-fourth year. "Where is your luggage?"

"It went down with the ferry, Auberon. Had we better just leave it?"

"Most certainly not."

The Major prided himself on his powers of organization. Mrs. Tooth sat peacefully in the sun while he directed the work of salvage, and on his return to shore with the sodden valises, her shoes, stockings and dress were once again dry.

"How did this happen?" she mildly inquired when the Major had settled her in his car. "I could get nothing from Dermot. Was it an earthquake?"

"No," was the grim reply. "An explosion."

"Somebody must have been very careless."

"It was deliberate. And we have strong suspicions who did it, too," he told her. "But no one speaks of it here, lest the ruffians blow them up as well."

"It seems rather the thing today," Mrs. Tooth concurred. "There was a bomb on the railway line to Camogli a month ago, we never heard why. What other news have you for me?"

The Major was only too willing to satisfy her. "Roger has gone off his chump," he began. "Last time I saw him, he gave me water to drink with something noxious in it. Luckily I spat it out at once, or he would have poisoned me. I haven't seen him again."

"It does sound very unbalanced," said Mrs. Tooth. "Of course I hardly know him, but he always struck me as unusually level-headed. And how are those dear children, Sabina and Thomas? I had a card from her at Christmas, she never forgets."

The Major's account of affairs at Mount Skellin came as near to jolting her out of her calm as anything could. "I am sorry indeed to hear that," she exclaimed. "It is always a great mistake to let family property go. If Thomas wished to be rid of the place, he could have made it over to Sabby. And what does he mean to do with himself, once it is gone?"

"That is what nobody knows," the Major said darkly. "And no one even knows where he is, except the English boy who has bought him out. Now, here's the extraordinary thing. I went up to see young Thomas the morning he disappeared, and the English boy said nothing about his buying the place. Then I went on to see Sabina, and *she* said nothing about it, either. She was most unhelpful, not at all like herself. I detest gossip, never will listen, but I only got the story from the postman. But Sabina knew of the sale, because the night before, she was heard to call the English boy a grabber in Moriarty's bar."

"Sabina in a bar!" cried Mrs. Tooth. "And calling people names!"

"Yes, what is one to make of it? And the servant I spoke to at Mount Skellin knows more than she will admit. She spun two different yarns to me about poor Thomas. First, he was having breakfast; then he was she-didn't-know-where, but he hadn't slept in his bed. And Sabina shrugged it all off. Rang up the stationmaster, who said Thomas had left on the morning train. And nothing has been heard of him since."

Mrs. Tooth pondered these facts for a while. "It is certainly strange," she decided presently. "And the Englishman—what sort of a person is he?"

"Oh, pleasant enough, well spoken, a Sahib, all that," the Major conceded. "But very much in the saddle, quite the young master. Practically showed me the door when I started putting questions. A bit of a dark horse. Because, look here—of all places in the world, why choose to pick on this?" It was what he in fact had done himself, but it seemed to throw a sinister light on Buckle. "A rum go altogether," he said in conclusion. "Rum as can be."

On reaching Capri Heights, Mrs. Tooth was confronted with further instances of change. To begin with, instead of bonny smiling Peg, fairy of the hearth for the past five years, she was faced by a younger sister, on the verge of tears and sorely in need of a handkerchief. Nothing was ready, for Mrs. Tooth's letter had arrived only an hour before herself, and in any case

Peg's successor had no idea where things were kept or what to do. Peg was gone to London and at work in a factory, said the sniffling child, whose age Mrs. Tooth assessed at eleven: Mammy had sent her up instead and she would do her best for the lady, only she wasn't wise, not like Peg.

"Let me see, I think you must be Polly," said Mrs. Tooth— Polly had figured largely in Peg's conversation, as a useless lump and a slut. "Well, Polly, it was most kind and thoughtful of your mother to send you, and you must please be sure to thank her for me." Polly wound one grubby leg round the other and dried her nose on her sleeve.

While the Major went to the kitchen to try and start a fire, Mrs. Tooth toured the house, opening the windows to air and sun. Everything was in order and as she expected. The heaters had failed, as they always did, and the shoes in her wardrobe were covered with green mold. Peg's brother had kept his word and painted the porch a glossy white, not forgetting an umbrella inadvertently left in the stand. Cobwebs were rife, mouseholes yawned, insects in astonishing profusion and variety lay dead on the floors. It was delightful to be home again, among the familiar comforting things.

But presently from an upstairs room she glanced out over her meadow, and what she saw sent her hurrying down in search of Major Floud. Aware of her vagueness, slow to think ill of others, she was always doubtful of anything which seemed amiss. Returning, on the famous occasion, to find her Bentley picked clean, she was half disposed to believe she had left it in that condition; and another time, when builders had been at work in her absence, she quite imagined that five dozen empty bottles on the Chippendale in her drawing room and innumerable cigarette stubs on her carpet were there by an oversight of her own. Unwilling, therefore, to leap to conclusions now, she went in search of another, more solid opinion.

"Auberon," she said, "I know I am very silly, but I always imagined I had two cows and that they were red."

The Major welcomed a relief in his struggles with the fire. Paper, kindling, turf and matches, all were damp as could be; the chimney was cold; and Polly sat on a chair beside him, drawing a long, lugubrious sniff every thirty seconds.

"Quite right, m'dear, so you have," he assured Mrs. Tooth, straightening up and caressing the small of his back. "Two fine Herefords."

"But there is only one in the meadow and it is black."

The Major walked across to the window and verified her statement. "Bless my soul, what can be up?" he cried. "That's Roger's Kerry."

"How very odd," said Mrs. Tooth. "Of course I have no objection, but it seems very odd."

"No odder than trying to poison me," the Major tartly observed.

"But what has become of my own two cows?" asked Mrs. Tooth. "Surely the Colonel hasn't driven them off? A British Army officer?"

"I'd put nothing past him," was the reply. "But have you no one looking after them?"

Mrs. Tooth communed with herself awhile. "Yes, I have," she then announced. "And a most dependable youth he is. Tim Foley."

The Quiet End of Evening

"Tim Foley—the Sergeant's son?" said the Major, aghast. "But he went to England months ago. After the New Year. He came to say good-bye and had I any old shoes to spare."

"I hope he didn't take my cows with him, then," said Mrs. Tooth with concern. "One hears such terrible things about the mailboat."

"I ought to have kept an eye on them," the Major said glumly. "He's probably passed them on to a cousin. What arrangement did you have?"

It appeared that Mr. Foley received no wages, but sold the milk and put a weekly stamp on his card, enabling him to draw the dole throughout the summer.

"Here, you, nip down to Foley's and ask where Mrs. Tooth's cows have got to," commanded the Major. "D'you hear me?" he said as Polly, trembling, sat rooted to her chair.

"I daresay she knows where they are herself," said Mrs. Tooth benignly. "You are not afraid of us, are you, Polly? Of course not."

Polly was frightend almost out of her wits. She had been thoroughly briefed on this matter at home and rehearsed as to what she must say, but it was one thing to repeat the words, parrotlike, after her mammy and quite another to bring them out with the Major's sharp little eyes boring grimly into hers.

"Oh, ma'am!" she faltered. "Oh, ma'am!"

"Well?" barked the Major.

Polly broke into helpless tears. "I wasn't to tell it, ma'am," she sobbed. "But Timo did sell them at the fair, the week before he went away."

"Sold them at the fair!" cried Major Floud. "Rosemary, did you sanction this?"

"No," she replied, "not as far as I remember."

"And what has he done with the money?" the Major continued, rounding on Polly again. "Is it here in the house or did he bank it?"

It was some little while before Polly could be made to understand the question, and longer still before a reply was, by gradual stages, elicited. Then it emerged that Mr. Foley had seen the transaction in a peculiar, but not illogical, light of his own. Having decided to go to England, he would not be able to draw the dole in Ireland that summer and the monies accruing from the sale of the cows were therefore applied to his uses, in compensation.

"He said how you'd never miss it," Polly concluded, weeping. "But don't tell me mammy 'twas I let on."

Mrs. Tooth promised to respect her confidence and comforted her as best she could, saying it was really of no importance. She was sorry the cows were gone, for they were lovely milkers, but gone they were and that was that. She had lived too long in the west to be possessive. And she would not hear of the Major's ramping down to Sergeant Foley, as he pined to do, for it would merely shame the poor man, guardian of the peace and upholder of the law, without recovering the cows.

"And if you work it out," she remarked with an air of wisdom, "what Tim must have got from the buyer would roughly amount to six months' dole. One cannot say he was greedy."

"You're far too soft, you spoil them all," the Major protested. "I'd be inclined to shoot the lot."

To console him for this frustration, Mrs. Tooth took him to the drawing room and gave him a glass of sherry while she resumed her tour of the house. Presently she was back with news of still more changes.

"I seem to have a neighbor," she said. "Someone has built a house at the end of the kitchen garden. On my side of the bank, what is more."

The Major fiercely drained his glass and set it down with a rap. "Rosemary, Rosemary, have you been had for a mug again?" he exploded. "Peadar MacGowan and his son built that, they were at it off and on all winter. I asked what they were doing and very cheeky they were. Told me nothing, but said it was on your instructions."

There was a pause while Mrs. Tooth assembled her powers of recall. "I did say something to Peadar one day about my needing a shed," she confessed. "That is quite true. But to the best of my belief, nothing was fixed. I am sure nothing was fixed. Of course, it had to be done sooner or later, but it is rather large. It will take the morning sun off the raspberries."

"Large!" cried the Major. "It's a cathedral!"

Mrs. Tooth was pleased with the notion. "Why, yes, a dear little mini cathedral," she said, laughing. "In fact, with a spire or two and some flying buttresses it might be a model of Chartres. How amazingly clever the people are here! They can turn their hand to anything. But it will throw rather a shadow on the fruit, until the sun is high."

"And Peadar's account will throw rather a shadow when you get it," the Major retorted sourly. "A shed, indeed! But they are all the same—hooks, every mother's son."

Mrs. Tooth did not argue, but she privately felt that Peadar had saved her a deal of trouble and, sociable woman that she was, it was still a relief to find no resident strangers in her garden. She made haste to replenish the Major's glass, took one for herself, and sitting down, turned the conversation on other things.

"And so we live on an island now," she began. "I find that most romantic."

The Major set to work to correct this view, listing the inconveniences already caused by the patriots' action and forecasting others to result from the loss of the ferry. "There's only one good thing about it," he declared. "It has frightened the beastly tourists away."

"But they were always so anxious for tourists to come here," said Mrs. Tooth. "What can have happened to change their minds? Of course we don't get the class of people we formerly did, but pray, who does? I hardly knew Rapallo."

"Oh, it isn't that. They never see further than the end of their noses," he explained. "It was a protest of some sort, against the Government. Or so I hear. There was some idea of declaring themselves a sovereign state, with their own flag and currency."

"Their own currency too! That does sound rather extreme. What would they do with it?"

"Devalue, I gather," was the bleak reply. "To bolster the economy. But I fancy it's all hot air."

Polly came in, her spirits restored, to say the fire wouldn't be lighting. Mrs. Tooth hurried out to see to matters herself, musing as she did so on the various disclosures of Auberon Floud. On her return she spoke in brisker, more decided tones than he was wont to hear.

"This is a bad business about Mount Skellin," she said, "but something may perhaps be done. Naturally, Sabina must be consulted. But first of all, indeed now, we will patch up your little tiff with Roger. We cannot afford dissension among ourselves."

"Little tiff! I tell you, the blackguard tried to poison me!" the Major cried.

"May you not have misunderstood him?"

"How? He insisted I drink the water—I don't like water, never touch the stuff—and there was something in it. Something filthy. I couldn't get the taste away for hours."

"He must have had a reason," Mrs. Tooth maintained. "I have heard of his dogs attacking people, but never of him. And you are his best friend."

"I was," said the Major sourly. "But the long and the short of it is, he's off his chump. I never pass the bungalow but he's fitting a new lock or setting up more barbed wire or digging a hole for someone to fall into and break their legs. And he has electrified the gate. I hear the postman is going to sue. And yet you talk of patching things up!"

"Yes, I do," said Mrs. Tooth. Like other gentle, yielding souls, on occasion she was as determined as a mule. "He has always done the things you mention, poor man. They are his pastimes. I do wish he cared for gardening. Or embroidery— there was an admiral in Rapallo who did petit point most delightfully. Could we interest the Colonel in jigsaw puzzles? I have an enormous one of the Taj Mahal, which would probably take him the rest of his life."

Despite all Major Floud could argue further, they were presently in his car again, speeding along the road to Simla. But I shall demand that apology at least, he thought. And in writing.

As things turned out, he got no chance to do so or to speak at all to any purpose. A new Colonel confronted the visitors, galvanized, febrile, bursting with pent-up talk. The arrival of the oilmen, their visit to himself, the questions they put and the investigations they carried out, and their protracted stay on Inishnamona, had confirmed his wildest hopes. He was in the blissful state of mind where every circumstance only seems to prove the wished-for case. That the men had left without another word to him, for example, showed their findings to be so important as to call for discussion on the highest level. The miracle had happened, his life would be transformed: already he saw himself, rejuvenated, hunting with the Kildares, shooting tiger in Bengal, boating in Kashmir or reading the papers in an exclusive London club.

One reference only was made to the incident which had so alienated the Major. "That is why I wished you to drink that water, Auberon," the Colonel said. "To taste the oil in it for yourself. Tasting is believing. I tried it out on young Boxham and he was convinced directly."

"Young Boxham has disappeared," the Major said, as if there might be some connection.

But the Colonel was off again regardless, while the others harkened in consternation. At last he talked himself dry and leaned back in his chair, beatifically grinning.

"I tell you, young Boxham has vanished," the Major repeated. "And Mount Skellin is sold."

"And so will Simla be, before long!" chortled the Colonel.

"Hang it, Roger, you might take an interest. Have you heard anything of Sabina?"

"No. Yes. She came in a couple of days ago, now I think of it," was the offhand reply. "To borrow a gun."

"A gun!" echoed Mrs. Tooth. "Why did she want it?"

"How should I know? To shoot with, I fancy. That's what guns are for," the Colonel pointed out. "I showed her how to load it—she cottoned on very well. Thousand pities she wasn't a boy, I always think."

But his mind was plainly fixed on his own affairs and soon the visitors took their departure.

"Raving mad," said the Major.

"But happy," said Mrs. Tooth. "Dear me, the excitement! We are an island, the ferry is sunk, Tom has vanished, Sabina is drinking in bars and borrowing guns. There's no place like home. But we really must save Mount Skellin, you know. By the way, how shall I manage for dinner?"

"Better have it with me," the Major replied. "You'll get nothing anywhere else. Soon there will be nothing to be had at all. Worse than war in the desert. Bloody Sinn Feiners! Shoot the lot, I say." And his grim face softened a little with pleasure as he pictured the scene to himself.

Fourteen

THE FINE WEATHER HAD CONTINUED, and Sabina grew daily more obsessed by her longing for a deep hot bath. Everything had fallen out exactly as she expected, and all was still to do. The new bath lay where Twomey's men had dropped it, in the garden, side by side with its derelict predecessor. Until it was installed the pump could not be used, for fear of inundation. The rain barrel being dry, every drop of water must be drawn from the well by hand, transferred from pail to pot and heated on the stove. It all took so much time that other activities were superseded, and what should have been the background to life turned into life itself: the day was a round of makeshifts and expedients and chores that never ended, winding up with a squalid piecemeal wash in a plastic tub.

By now Peadar MacGowan's turf was cut and once or twice she ran him to earth, always to hear the old assurances, uttered with all the old sincerity as he looked her in the eye, frank and unflinching. He was delayed on a job, long promised, just at the moment, but he would be up to her without fail in the morning; if his own wishes counted at all, he'd have been there long since. This pursuit, capture, demand and response had become a ritual devoid of any significance, but she observed it, as empty rituals are observed, because its cessation would leave a gap in life.

Sabina had long ago and, she thought, for good, made up her mind on all concerning Ireland and its people. The lies that tripped so sweetly off Peadar's tongue, the promises given without a thought and broken without a pang, she had laid at England's door. Such things were the sole, therefore the legitimate, defense of the weak against the strong. But now she began to toy with a hypothesis which, though far from new and to the likes of her brother self-evident, had struck her mind with all the force and surprise of revelation. What if all this while she had been putting the cart before the horse? What if Irish character were to blame for Irish history, and not the other way round? What, in a nutshell, if the people were not and never had been any damn good at all and had asked for, merited, whatever they got?

A stranger seemed to have rented part of her mind and to be playing the deuce with its furniture. And then, as if to shame her, Peadar turned up one morning out of the blue with a bag of tools on his arm and a mop-headed boy to assist him. Gay and self-possessed, he announced he would have the old bath sorted and herself afloat before he'd eat his dinner. But first he took from the bag a teapot, with tea and sugar mixed inside, and begged her to wet it for him, saying he hadn't been able to take his breakfast at home for thinking of her. From the way he spoke, one might have thought that news of her trouble had only just reached him and that he had instantly dropped all else to fly to the rescue.

Overjoyed, Sabina ran to put on a kettle, reproaching herself for her cruel, unfounded thoughts. The people always turned up trumps, in their own good time and when it was least expected, just as after weeks and weeks of relentless rain the sky would suddenly clear, the sun break out and a huge double rainbow span the sea. Her bath would be all the more delicious after the long period of deprivation. But as she waited for the water to boil, the telephone began to ring in the shrill, vehement way it had when the postmistress wanted to speak herself, and she lifted the receiver with a grim foreboding.

"Is Peadar MacGowan at you, Miss Boxham?"

"He is."

"We're after getting word from the hospital, his mother-in-law is dead."

At times it was difficult not to feel that the devil himself was stalking through Inishnamona. Sabina could have wept and torn her hair. Why had she not left the telephone to tire itself out with ringing? What difference could an hour or so make to Peadar, who was so little fond of his mother-in-law as to have celebrated her removal by the ambulance with a three-day skite? But now, whatever his personal views, custom required him to stop work at once and do no more until the funeral was over. Three days were lost—one for the wake, one for the body to go to the church, one for the requiem and the burial—not to speak of the junketings to follow, when the neighbors who dug the grave and carried the coffin were suitably rewarded for their assistance.

There was no help for it, however, and she brought him the news with his tea.

"And herself due for the pinsion next month!" he remarked bitterly, putting the tools away.

"I'll see you on Thursday, will I?" Sabina asked, her eagerness too much for her manners.

"Thursday . . . well, Thursday is a holy day, Miss Boxham."

So it was: Corpus Christi. Not a tap to be done by a soul.

"On Friday, then?" she persisted, trying to keep the irritation out of her voice.

But on Friday the bishop would visit to confirm the children, among them Peadar's youngest, and on Saturday the local hurling team, of which he was a valued member, would meet Ballycagey. Then followed Sunday, day of rest and drink, and with the emotional stresses of the week behind him he would hardly be fit for work before Wednesday at the earliest—by which time he would have completely forgotten Miss Boxham and her bathtub.

Hope deferred is as nothing to hope on the point of fulfillment and then dashed to the ground, after all; and when Peadar had gone, Sabina made a momentous decision. Momentous, that is, as the thing transpired, because in itself it could not have seemed more harmless and banal: she would go at once to Mount Skellin and have a bath there, in one of its seven bathrooms. Like a person famished who dreams of food rather than of ways to get it, she thought only of the steaming water, the voluptuous warmth, the fragrance of soap, of limbs recently so parched and pallid turning moist and pink. Those pleasant matters filled her mind completely as she drove the trap along, her sponge bag packed and ready at her side. Finn knew the way too well to need instruction, and when all at once he stopped short, it took her a moment or two to realize that he had done this and what his reasons were.

The high beautiful wrought-iron gates at the entrance to the park were shut. In all her life she had never seen them shut, had hardly supposed them capable of shutting. There they had always stood, open and inviting, like tutelary deities guarding the approach to a temple. To find the way thus barred was disagreeable enough in itself, but what was worse, it brought home, rubbed in, the awful changes in her own position. She was now, in her childhood's home and that of her forebears, a visitor, a guest, and one with a favor to ask: "Would you be kind enough to let me have a bath here, Mr. Buckle? Those wretches have still not attended to mine."

How could she address these words to a man whom, at their last meeting, she had stigmatized as a grabber? If it came to that, how was she even to make her presence known to him? The English, she understood, did not walk into people's houses and bawl for them in the friendly Irish fashion. Must she knock at the door, wait for Maggie or Bridie to open, send in her name and ask for the courtesy of an interview? And if this was granted, could she come straight to the point of the bath, without first making an apology for the insult hurled at Mount Skellin's new master the other day?

The probable humiliations were numerous and varied. Sabina was half inclined to wheel about and start for home, but then she considered her bath. As Stendhal, with Moscow in flames and the *Grande Armée* retreating, thought principally of his raging toothache, so did Sabina ignore her graver distresses to dwell on her sticky, unwashed condition.

She decided to sneak into the house by one of the many doors, make her way to the remotest of the bathrooms and sneak out again, with no one a penny the wiser. She would enter by the rear, trotting on to Starlight Point and turning up the shady track that led to Norah Malone's. Halfway up, screened from the road by the mountain ash that grew on either bank, she would tether Finn and cross the bog on foot to the boundary of the estate. Here was a bosky of stunted firs extending to the orchards, which went as far as the stables; after that she had cover all the way.

There was no fear, she reckoned, of anyone passing up or down and wondering what Miss Boxham's trap was doing, abandoned in the wilds. Norah Malone was an aged woman who never left her fireside but for mass, wakes and funerals. The traveling shops that supplied her frugal needs called only in the afternoon. Dano, the postman, came in the morning to collect any mail she had, bring her the news and establish that she was still alive, but Dano must have gone his way an hour before and more.

Sabina's plan was reasonable and foolproof and, as such, unsuited to the rhythms of Inishnamona life. Dano was late, for once through no fault of his own. Sometime before, a company of agricultural purveyors had marketed a weed-killer of deadly strength which they supplied in large, unwieldy drums, and the people on their tiny holdings found it easier to decant this fluid into any smaller vessel that came to hand. More often than not, the makeshift container was an empty whiskey bottle with the label still left on, and this, in a community both convivial and absent-minded, had led to an alarming number of deaths. The company had admonished their retailers in the strongest terms, but without appreciable results, and it was now resolved on sending a personal note to every householder in the region, including some who had left for England or were dead these fifty years. Today poor Dano's bag was heavy with their appeals, objects of derision which the law obliged him, nonetheless, to deliver. To pause by Miss Boxham's trap, to meditate on the mystery of its being there, to speculate on the owner's whereabouts and to conceive various lively interpretations of the whole affair made a welcome break in what promised to be a day of unrelieved exertion.

Of this Sabina was, naturally, unaware. Comforting Finn with words and caresses, she tied his reins to a tree and crossed the bog, threading her way among dry gulches and gullies, slipped through the orchards with their protective cloud of blossom, skirted the stables and barns, and shot in at the scullery door. Here she had the choice of traversing the kitchen to reach the hall and the main stairway or of by-passing it down a flagged corridor with interior windows facing on it. Luckily she took the second course, for, glancing through one of these windows, she was halted in her tracks by the sight of Buckle, an apron around his waist, busy with a frying pan at the stove. It turned her hot and cold to think how easily she might have burst in upon him, sponge bag in hand, towel over her arm. What could he, in God's name, be up to?

Now he broke a couple of eggs into the pan and carefully basted them with fat, as intent on his work as a child. There was something appealing about the young man as he stood there, so grave and engrossed, so unconscious of the enemy within his walls. Evidently he had waited in vain for his breakfast and was now preparing one for himself. That was it: Maggie and Bridie had gone to the wake for Peadar's mother-in-law, without a word of explanation, for fear the Englishman would laugh at their primitive customs. And no doubt, Sabina told herself, working up to resist the attractive impression he made, no doubt he would laugh at them, too, laugh their simple pieties to scorn. And no doubt he expected, like all the English, to find a household of serfs there, without wills of their own or human rights, who would fly to do his bidding, wait on him hand and foot and call him "Your Honor." Splendid! He would very soon learn better, and learn it the hardest way.

Smiling grimly, her momentary weakness overcome, she sped down the passage and up one of the back flights of stairs to the shelter of the bathroom, so far from the danger zone that she could, if she liked, sing at the top of her lungs as she washed.

The room was huge, with a marble floor and a nineteenth-century bathtub like a sarcophagus, which rested on three iron paws and a brick, the remaining paw having dropped away. The door could not be locked, as the key was missing, nor even shut, as the handle revolved idly without engaging the tongue, but it was a massive piece of timber, sufficiently heavy to stay where she pushed it. By great good fortune—as the bath was never used —the plug was still there, but Sabina did not put it in at once, knowing it would take the hot water some little time to travel up so far. Seating herself on the curved rim of the bath, she turned on the tap and waited.

First came the familiar gush of dark-brown water, earwigs

and spiders, accompanied by a rumble, as of distant thunder. Gradually the water cleared and the torrent of insects ceased, although the rumble continued as before. Presently the flow grew warm, then hot, then scalding, and Sabina thrust in the stopper. The rumble swelled to a mighty roar, like that of an express train, and the pipes moaned and shuddered as if in sympathy: indeed, the very house appeared to be in convulsion. Somewhat taken aback, Sabina turned off the hot water as soon as it was deep enough and started the cold, which merely added a piercing scream to the concerto. At last her bath was ready. Throwing off her clothes, she stepped in with gasps of delight, while the hullabaloo in the water system dwindled away to a series of half-hearted hiccups.

Humming an old Irish air, she soaped and scrubbed, splashed and wallowed. But after a few minutes she was conscious of a new draft, other than those from the window and chimney, playing on her back. The room was so full of steam that she could hardly see across it, but peering through the mist, she just made out that the door was standing open and the figure of a man loomed up toward her, and before she had time to collect her wits the man spoke, with the voice of Harry Buckle.

"I say," he cheerfully remarked, "how awfully nice to see you."

It is doubtful, in the circumstances, that anything he said would have endeared him much to Sabina, but these particular words filled her with rage. "How dare you!" she cried, rolling herself into a ball for the sake of decorum. "Have you no decency whatsoever?"

Buckle was hurt by this inquiry. "How could I know it was you?" he pleaded. "There was an extraordinary noise in the plumbing—a new one, to me—and I tracked it here. The door wasn't shut and I came in. What's so indecent? All I can see, and that indistinctly, is the back of your head and your shoulders. I have seen more at the London Opera."

"No doubt!" snapped Miss Boxham with loathing. "Will you kindly leave the room at once?"

Mr. Buckle firmly stood his ground. "Are you still at war with me, then?" he asked. "To come here without making your presence known and help yourself to a bath strikes me as rather a friendly thing to do. I, at any rate, should not have done so to anyone I disliked."

"I won't argue," Sabina said, but somewhat lamely, feeling the force of his words. "Go away, I do beg."

"No, I shan't," Mr. Buckle replied with spirit. "I have been wanting to talk to you, and this seems as good a chance as I shall get. Please understand how things are."

"Do you call yourself a gentleman?" came in withering tones.

"No. Where was I? Please understand how things are. I shall be buying something I badly want, that your brother badly wants to sell. That's all about it. Thomas is to be as much at home as ever here, and my hope is that you will be the same. Dear Sabina—"

"Don't call me Sabina."

"Dear Sabina," Buckle repeated while she writhed in helpless fury, "do be reasonable. Since Thomas wishes to sell, why not to me as much as to anyone else? Would you rather see the place a convent or a hotel?"

"Yes—any day."

"I wonder," he remarked a little dryly. "And I wonder, too, what I have done to incur such hostility."

"You stand there and ask that!" Sabina was trembling all over.

"I will let you into a secret," Mr. Buckle continued, busy with his thoughts. "Perhaps I shouldn't, but I will. You are to share the purchase money, half and half. Thomas is resolved on that."

Far from appeasing her, the disclosure made her wild. The more he said in mitigation of her grievance, the more she hugged it to her bosom; and this final, calm, so English, supposition that money would bring her around was past enduring. Nor could she endure a second longer the mortification of being held his captive. In a sudden frenzy she bounded from the bath and confronted him, too furious for shame.

"Now," she panted, "will you leave the room at last?"

We read in Irish history of a Gaelic rout accomplished by these means. The valiant Cuchulain advanced, invincible, until crafty Maeve of Connaught sent naked women forth to meet him, at which the hero wavered, overcome with confusion, and turned aside. Whether Miss Boxham had this precedent in mind or not, she certainly expected Mr. Buckle to retire at once in consternation. Nothing in her experience enabled her to conceive of any other course. But Harry Buckle, though chaste enough by present-day standards, was not an ancient Gael. He was London and contemporary to the core. Exposed female flesh held no terrors for him, nor even the charms of novelty; indeed, to tell the truth, he was just a little wearied of it.

At this particular moment, however, his reaction was one of simple, friendly concern. "By all means, if you really wish me to," he said. "But you mustn't stand about, do get your togs on. Nothing strikes upward like a marble floor, and the drafts in here are shocking." He looked around, saw the towel and passed it to her. "You don't drink, I know," he resumed in this nannyish strain, "but I shall leave a cordial for you in the library. And next time you come, do pray use another bathroom. There are seven to choose from, after all. No need to plump for the coldest of the lot!" With that, he bowed politely and went away.

Sabina flung her clothes on and tore from the house as if the furies were after her. Nothing so ignominious had ever happened in all her life. The memory of it seared her mind with an almost physical pain. Buckle's words echoed obsessively in her ears— cool, calm, conciliatory, driving her to distraction. It was not until she was on the road, urging poor Finn by voice and whip to a canter, that one of the phrases he had used came back with a sudden promise of hope. "I shall be buying something I badly want," he had said, not "I have bought . . ." Nothing, then, was as yet irrevocably fixed, and with a little assistance from her, Mr. Buckle might change his plans even now.

Never one to let the grass grow under her feet, she called on Colonel Sentence forthwith, to ask for the loan of a gun and instruction in its use. He asked no questions and was only too pleased to comply; in his opinion, the more Sahibs who could handle firearms, the better. Sabina went home feeling happier than she had for many a day, hid the gun—a rifle—in the turf shed and proceeded, as her duty was, to the wake at Peadar MacGowan's.

Fifteen

WITH THE SINKING OF THE FERRY, affairs on Inishnamona went
from awkward to impossible. All ideas of attracting tourists had
to be shelved, since God alone knew how the people themselves
were to manage. Food and drink grew scarce, every vehicle left
the road, and what little employment there was came to a halt.
The drift to England turned into a headlong rush, and when
Peadar MacGowan joined it, leaving his age-old projects all in the
air, it seemed as if the Book of Life itself were closed.

Nevertheless, a certain breed of strangers continued to
trickle in, a breed that nothing could frighten away. These were
the Yanks, so called to distinguish them from "rale" Americans,
those who had plenty of money and were willing to spend it.
Yanks were frugal, tightwads even, descendants of local people
who had emigrated after the Famine and before England succeeded the States as their El Dorado. Their principal occupation
was to poke about the briars and brambles of some derelict grave-

yard, ancestor hunting, much as children comb a beach for winkles and whelks.

At the best of times they were unpopular, to an extent which might have startled them had they suspected it; and indeed it is hard to imagine why they were, unless their tireless boasting about America and unsparing comments on local life—with peculiar emphasis on the sanitation—had something to do with the matter. But they were tolerated because, although on the spot they found the Irish backward, bigoted and unhygienic, once home in America they apparently derived the greatest comfort from the fact of being Irish themselves. Closefisted they might be on holiday, but back in their own surroundings they never failed to support an Irish enterprise as long as it sounded worthy, a condition which was simple enough to fulfill. In the belief that they were establishing a youth club, promoting fireside industry and fostering Gaelic culture, Yanks of Inishnamona descent had built onto Moriarty's Lounge, provided O'Shea with his van and set Micky Malone up in greyhounds.

But, as stated, they were still at the best of times not loved, and at times like the present they would have done well to lie low and keep mum. Unhappily, this seemed the last thing a Yank could do. To a man they felt the need, one might really say the morbid craving, to express their views and communicate their ideas; and the remarks—provocative, facetious or scathing—which they were apt to pass about the local patriots and their misguided protest, beggar description.

Had they been content only to voice their thoughts in the pubs, among men, it would not have mattered so much. There would have been arguments, perhaps a brawl, but custom required, with all the power of common law behind it, that anything said or done in drink be forgotten by morning. The trouble was, they dinned their views into the ears of the women, who shared them already and were zealous in passing them on. Yanks seldom used the hotels, even when these were open, but preferred to billet themselves on the natives, feeling that in this way they got nearer the grass roots and were saving money as well. There they would sit and prate, with the folkish tweed hats supplied by Twomey pushed to the back of their heads, while the woman of the house boiled her potatoes or scrubbed her floor: they were worse than twenty children. Or they would accost some perfect stranger along the road and launch into one of their monologues, making their predictable points over and over, wholly unmoved by signs of distress and impatience. As Pio Moriarty said, a dog would strike his father to hear them.

But the scourge had other effects beyond simply enraging the men and goading the women. It helped to crystallize those thoughts which had been forming in the keener local intellects for a considerable length of time. Even before the ferry sank, there had been the pensive looks when allusion was made to the famous exploit; afterward all mention of it ceased, except that Pio often dwelt on the wake which had kept him unavoidably absent on the occasion itself.

No one, even now, went so far as to declare it a blunder— no one spoke of the past at all—but there was a growing recognition that something would have to be done about the present. And with that recognition came the dawn of a political instinct. The patriots sensed that whether history would acclaim or condemn them, the initiative now must pass to other hands. "Discredited" was perhaps too harsh a word to use, but the patriots were positively not the prime favorites with the folk in general. What they needed was fresh blood, new ideas—any ideas, indeed, for they had none—a man with the interests of Inishnamona at heart but who had taken no part in the action, if possible had even denounced it. The priest would have suited them well, anticlerical though they mostly were, but Father Kelly was much too sharp to land himself in their pickles and, moreover, had fish of his own to fry.

Their choice, then, fell on Brother Expeditus, up at the monastery, one of three surviving inhabitants and a jolly, active fellow of sixty-odd. In the eyes of Brother Cyril and Brother John, whose ages totaled one hundred and seventy-four, he was a mere sprig, but he was a traveled, educated man, full of schemes and projects. Once upon a time the community had earned their living by making cheese, of the raw flavor and soapy texture agreeable to the Irish palate; but when Brother Expeditus joined them they blossomed out under his guidance into all kinds of fancy stuff, to which they gave such romantic names as Camembert, Fromage Monsieur, Pont 'l'Evêque and Brie, until certain foreign interests threatened to sue and the French ambassador called on the Taoiseach. By then they had lost their old customers and acquired no others. Death was gradually depleting their ranks, age enfeebling those who were left; the monastery sold its ominous trademark and phantom good will to some innocent nuns in Kerry and turned to contemplation.

Nowadays it performed no public service at all, unless the ringing of the Angelus could be so described. That duty devolved on Brother Expeditus, as Brother John never knew the time of day and Brother Cyril could only count to twelve; but although he discharged the task with zeal, it left his energies unabsorbed. He was forever thinking of ways and means whereby the fortunes of the monastery could be revived and the community rebuilt. Like the patriots, Brother Expeditus was a man with a dream: he loved to imagine the rise of a great Catholic center attracting pilgrims from every part of Europe and offering them holy relics, postcards and lunches at Dublin rates; but his efforts to make that dream a fact were, like theirs, prone to miscarry.

The last of a long series of schemes was the most original and also the most spectacular. Apart from turf, the most abundant natural resource of the region was seaweed, and from this the friar proposed to distill a liqueur that would vie, among the cognoscenti, with Bénédictine and Chartreuse. He was busy for months before the results were to his satisfaction and he felt ready to offer them to the world. A gala was held at Moriarty's, with an extension to three o'clock, meaning half past four. People came from far and wide—the girls with strange African hairdos and Milo Twomey toilettes, and there was a minister fellow down from Dublin dishing out guff about the renascent west which the *Bugle* printed the next day on page one with a photograph—but there was no masking the fact that the fluid, handed around in little ceremonial nips after the prayers and blessings and speeches and before the serious drinking began, was common, or garden, poteen with salt and coloring added. Nothing was said, for no one wanted to hurt the poor man's feelings after he had worked so long, but the product never reached the market. Rumors went flying about as usual: it was said that the Guards had been up at the monastery and taken away the worm and the still, and that Rome had laid an inhibition on Brother Expeditus himself, but the monastery kept its secrets well and nothing was ever known.

Pio had always been for Brother Expeditus after he put that nice little bit of business his way, and now he volunteered to approach him. Early the next morning he found the friar on the shore near the monastery lands, bent double, hauling on a couple of ropes as if in a tug of war.

"Give us a hand here, Pio," the Brother called, panting. He was short and chubby, with a shock of white hair, a rosy, smiling face and the candid eyes of a child. "If we haven't an eight-pound salmon caught, I'll eat the net itself. And I nearly could—divil a bite of Christian food did we see since the ferry went. So yesterday when the tide was out I said a prayer and laid the net, and let's see now what God put in it for us."

They hauled and heaved and at last the net began to move sluggishly. What God, inscrutably, had favored the Brothers with, was a dogfish five foot long, bushels of seaweed and hundreds of tiny crabs.

"Teach us to adore Thy holy will," the friar prayed. "A nice bloody mess the net's in. That'll take me a week to clean and mend. And I still don't know what to put on the table for dinner. Porridge again, I suppose—Brother John's going to be as cross as a bear."

Pio felt the moment propitious for coming to the point of his visit without the usual circumlocutions. Having condoled with the community's plight, he passed straight on to that of the island at large, while the Brother followed with warm interest, pensively rubbing the small of his back.

·"I'll have to think it out," he said. "It isn't a matter you'd want to rush, now is it? I don't just know what happens when people declare themselves an island and then feel continental again." A delicate man, he meant by this to remind the Chairman that the causeway was gone for good. "And if I do come up with something, I'd first have to consult with Brother John. Trouble is, he's as deaf as a beetle and won't wear an aid. Just like a woman, God forgive me; says everyone talks indistinctly these days and that his hearing was never better. But I'll do my best with him."

"That's the great man," said Pio. "Tell you what, me boys'll come back after school and clean the old net for you."

"Well, I won't refuse. If there's a job I hate! How are things your way?"

Pio's face darkened again to think of the prospects ahead. "There's stout for ten days, whiskey for maybe a whileen more," he said. "That's only if we don't get another wake. I dread to think of the future. The boys will tear the place apart once it's dry. I'd sooner deal with a pack of wolves than with some of them beauties."

"Offer it up," the friar suggested. "And who knows what mightn't come to pass before you even run dry at all? Maybe God will take a hand in the business. But I have to get back to the monastery now, before Brother Cyril would fall on the fire."

The holy man had taken to doing this of recent times, and also to cutting out photos of girls from the *Bugle* and pinning them up in his cell. Brother Expeditus sighed and shook his head. Brother Cyril was getting childish, so he was, God between him and all harm, but when you've no good to do you're as well to be gone.

"You'll see the old ones hanging on to life," the friar continued, "and the young cut off in their prime, like Mary O'Grady, God rest and reward her. And there poor Peadar was, giving her room all those years when he couldn't abide the thought of her, and then to have her whipped away a week before he'd get her pension! It's no wonder at all he went to England—he was about disgusted!" With that, having reached the monastery gates, he dropped the secular tone, imparted a blessing and promised again to do what lay in his power for Inishnamona's comfort.

But it was one thing to promise and quite another to carry out the promise. What could, in any circumstances, be done? Inishnamona was doomed. Lobster fishing would start any day, and there wouldn't be a boat for miles around to spare for anything else. There was a fair-sized packet that plied the outer islands, but these all had harbors of their own with good deep water; and anyhow, even if it were possible, nice fools they'd all look with a packet getting up steam to cross the eighty short yards!

The only solution that offered itself was a long-term one and fraught with difficulty, but it was grandiose enough to appeal to the friar's imagination. Taking their stand on their island status, the people must call on the Dublin crowd to build them a bridge, the same as they did in days gone by for Achill and, more recently, for Valentia. It would take years and cost millions, but it would have to come. The more he thought about it, the more he liked the idea. They'd want publicity, of course, sympathetic support from the press, but that wasn't a problem. Look how the

Bugle came running, the time they held that gala!

It was easy to gain the consent of Brother John, who only caught one word in seven and whose mind in any case was at present entirely fixed on food. Brother Expeditus lost no time in approaching the *Bugle*, nor the *Bugle* in sending a man to see him. The gala had been the finest story of that year and the prime office joke ever since. But as so often happens in dealings with the press, when Brother Expeditus read the account of his interview and the editorial comment on it, he barely recognized the material which with childlike trust he had heaped upon the reporter. In column after column the whole affair was treated as a gigantic lark: Inishnamona was held up to ridicule as the place where men blew up their roads and then clamored for bridges to help them out. Their hopes, their dreams, their aspirations, were laughed to scorn; comparison was made with the frog in the fable.

The island reeled under the blow, but worse was to come. The Dublin papers took it up, in the same spirit of heartless mockery; London followed suit, and then the capitals of Europe, and finally New York. Once more the eyes of the world were fastened on Inishnamona, but this time streaming with tears of laughter; and her people, on the brink of despair, writhed and raged and thirsted for revenge.

Sixteen

"I HAVE A SUGGESTION, Maggie," said Buckle to Maggie as she removed the luncheon things one day. "I am devoted to bacon and eggs. They are the glory of the Irish cuisine. And I cherish a fondness for puddings, white or black. Nevertheless, I should like to branch out a bit, add to the list, you know. How would it be if you sent up a stew, or some chops, or some fish? I hope you'll forgive my asking."

Maggie, and Bridie too, would have forgiven Mr. Buckle anything, if only because he could tell them apart. He was, indeed, unable to fathom how a normally observant eye could fail to do so. When a question was put to Maggie, she tilted her head to the left before she answered; when to Bridie, she moistened her lower lip with her tongue. When Maggie brought in the tray, she first set down the teapot, then the toast, hot water, bacon and eggs; Bridie did all this the other way around. That would have been enough, but there was more. Thomas had told him the twins remained identical because their lives, from birth on, had been uniformly dull, monotonous and devoid of event. Nothing had ever happened to one and not to the other, no separate experience to leave some mark of grief or joy. In spite of that, there were three or four gray hairs at each of Bridie's temples, on Maggie's head not one. Mr. Buckle could only conclude that poor Tom was short-sighted.

All the same, Maggie did now wear a somewhat offended look, but that was because she must disappoint him and hated to do it.

"I'd cook you anything in the world you wanted, Mr. Buckle," she assured him. "But what's a stew without the meat? There's none to be had, nor fish, and soon there won't be rashers and puddings. We'll have eggs while the chickens lay, but how long will that be? There's no more grain in the bin. We heard how some of the people are lifting the potatoes already, no bigger than marbles and without any goodness in them."

"Dear me," said Mr. Buckle. "This is due to the loss of the ferry, is it?"

"'Tis due to a crowd of stupid rascally bletherers," was the fierce reply, "that's after ruining the place and making us fools in front of them all. It was there on the *Bugle* last week, and what the *Bugle* might say today, the world would repeat tomorrow."

On the present occasion, at least, this was undoubtedly true.

"I must take in the *Bugle*, then," Mr. Buckle remarked. "But don't worry. I have a motorboat on order, and they have promised delivery this week. Then we can fend for ourselves, and until it comes we shall have to live off the land. I will try to shoot a rabbit this afternoon."

The Quiet End of Evening

"A rabbit, God help us!" cried Maggie in horror. "That's hardly fit for a gintleman's table!"

Disregarding this social comment, Mr. Buckle presently took his shotgun and made his way through the woods to a grassy dell where a tribe of rabbits had made its home.

Ahead of him there, with a similar object in mind, was the hero Barney Roche. Although he excelled as a marksman, as he did in all requiring keen sight and a steady nerve, he had brought no gun, judging it prudent to put down snares, which would make no noise. He intended to do so as a regular thing and to sell off the bag at prices in keeping with the shortage of food. It was not just the gentry for whose consumption rabbits were locally deemed unfit, the people despised them too, as they despised all manner of things enjoyed elsewhere: sweetbreads, kidneys, brains, oysters, crabs. But Barney reckoned they would have to overcome their aversion now, just as beleaguered cities are forced to live on dogs and rats. He meant to ask a starting price of seven-and-sixpence a skull and raise it from time to time as the famine grew, and he had prepared an account, should anyone call this procedure in question, of the miles he had to trudge and the hazards to undergo before he obtained his supplies.

He had hardly begun the work when he saw Mr. Buckle threading his way through the trees toward him, gun over arm. It was well for Barney that his eye was quick and alert, for the chattering of a stream overlaid the sound of footsteps, and in a few moments more Mr. Buckle would have been upon him. Had it been Mr. Thomas he would have greeted him pleasantly, talked of the lovely weather they were blessed with and how the same had inspired him to take a walk in the Skellin lands. Mr. Thomas would have known full well what brought him there, but like the Quality that he was, would have replied in suitable manner and left him to it. But Mr. Buckle was an enigma and no one knew how to take him. Why, for only one instance, had he shut those great front gates that no one in living memory had ever seen shut before?

The answer to that was straightforward enough. Buckle had swung them to one morning, out of curiosity to see if they could be moved at all, and having done so, found it beyond his powers to open them again. Needless to say, nothing so harmless and simple could ever occur to an Inishnamona mind. It must be, the new master was telling the people to keep away. It must be, he wished to have nothing to do with them. It must be, he was their enemy, as Colonel Sentence was, but the Colonel was old and crazy and Irish, and had lived among them for years. Mr. Buckle was not to suppose the people would swallow from him what they swallowed from Colonel Sentence.

Barney therefore looked on Mr. Buckle as a hostile force, now advancing upon him armed to the teeth. He flew to a nearby oak, rapidly scaled the trunk and settled himself in the fork of a branch. By this time the young spring leaves were all unfurled and a dense green curtain hid the ground from sight, and Barney felt sure, since he could not see Mr. Buckle, that Mr. Buckle could not see him.

But still his mind was far from easy. Nothing was to be heard but the prattling brook, the rustling leaves and now and again a burst from a cuckoo. He would not know when the coast was clear and it was safe for him to come down. For that matter, he was not so sure if he could come down at all. It is one thing to shin up a tree in a fright and another to descend in cold blood, as many a cat would confirm. Then, as he turned it all over dismally in his mind, the matter was settled for him, in a way he least expected. There came the bark of a gun and the *phtt!* of a bullet whizzing past his head, snapping a bough a bare nine inches away and sending leaves a-flutter to the ground.

So great was the shock that Barney fell from his perch, bumping from bough to bough as he went until he lay in the grass below, bawling that he was killed and dead. He kept this up with sustained, even mounting, vigor until he saw Mr. Buckle beside him, with a puzzled look on his face. Then he struggled into a sitting position and shook a fist at his assailant.

"I'll take you to court, you bloody murderer!" he yelled. "For all I'm on your land, you'd no right to fire. And didn't Mr. Boxham, God bless him, tell me come here whenever I'd be disposed? What's a rabbit to the likes of you, and the people starving? 'Twould melt a heart of stone to hear the little ones crying for food. And then to shoot a defenseless man, right through the head, before he'd have time to say a prayer! But aren't you the same as you always were, bloody murdering, grabbing British!"

With that he returned to a supine position, closed his eyes and gave vent to a series of blood-curdling groans.

"For a man shot through the head, you put your case very clearly," Mr. Buckle observed. "Particularly as you have had a nasty fall into the bargain. But you are wrong in thinking I fired at you. I had no idea there was anyone in the tree."

"Who fired the gun off, so? The fairies?" Barney inquired with sarcasm, opening his eyes again. "You can say all that to the Guards."

"Tut, man, that was a rifle and this is a shotgun," said Mr. Buckle. "Still fully loaded, too." He broke it and showed Barney Roche the two cartridges. "I'm as much at sea as you are."

"You had time to reload before you'd bother coming to look," retorted the implacable victim. "And don't be giving me fancy talk about rifles and shotguns. They're all the same, and if they weren't itself, it's no bloody odds to the one that's hit." He painfully got to his feet, stroked his head, worked his jaw and let out another groan. "You'll hear more of this, Mister bloody Englishman! There'll be thousands and thousands to pay!"

Wheeling about, he stalked toward the wood, caught his foot in a snare and measured his length again.

"So that was it," said Buckle severely. "Trapping is something I don't allow. Just take that up again, and any others you laid, then make yourself scarce. I am going after the rifleman."

But Barney lay where he was and went on groaning. "I'll never leave here on me own two feet," he lamented. "From the feel of me spine, I'd say it was fractured. And how's the ambulance to get across, with the ferry gone? They'll have to load me onto an ass, the way they did with Mollie Fizelle, and she expecting her ninth, and row to the other side with the sea raging all round. And after the shock and the pain of it, it's like enough I'd breathe me last before ever they'd drag the ass as far . . ."

How long, left to himself, he would have kept this threnody going is a matter of pure conjecture, for at this point the rifle barked again and another bullet tore whining into the branches

over his head. He was up in a flash and running for all he was
worth, cunningly zigzag, like a snipe, while Mr. Buckle turned
in the direction whence the bang had come and walked toward
it. The wood was too dense for bullets to fly singing through the
air: a tree would stop them short at once. The gunman was in the
dell. The only cover there was a massive boulder some little way
off at the brink of the stream. So the gunman must be behind it,
and as Mr. Buckle approached, it came to him also who that
gunman was.

"Come off it, Sabina, there's a dear," he called out with great
good humor, but with a touch of authority too. "Or I shall really
have to be cross with you!"

He quickened his pace as he spoke and was now some eighty
yards from the boulder. There was no reply, for Sabina cleared
the stream at a bound and flew like a hunted roe through the
wood, leaving gun and ammunition to the enemy. He picked up
the rifle and studied it: it was a good make but very old, and had
a number of notches on the butt. No doubt it belonged to
Thomas, but it was strange that he had never noticed it among
the well-cleaned, well-oiled shotguns that were the sole orderly
feature of the house.

When he went back to the gunroom again, he found only the
one empty stall in the rack. Flummoxed, he went in search of the
twins, who were drinking tea in the kitchen and brooding over
the latest issue of the *Bugle*.

"Do you happen to know where this comes from?" he asked,
holding out the rifle for their inspection. He had not expected
they would, but the answer came pat from both together.

"That's the Colonel's."

"Colonel Sentence?" Now, this was really odd! "I found it on the grass just now, near the wood, when I was looking for rabbits."

The twins communed with each other in silence, wondering how far they should inform him.

"I wouldn't think, sir, 'twas the Colonel that left it there," said Bridie, feeling her way.

"He's shocking careful with things that belong to him," said Maggie in support.

"You mean, someone stole it?"

"Ah, not at all!" cried Maggie, shocked by the very idea. "There's nothing stolen on Inishnamona!"

Bridie hastened to confirm that such indeed was the laudable fact. "You could never keep it dark," she pointed out. "'Tisn't like Manchester and all them places. Sure, you couldn't walk down the road here but everyone knew it, and why you were going, too."

"I've a notion you know rather more than you're letting on," Mr. Buckle observed, affable as he always was but with an English directness that disconcerted them. "For that matter, I do too. It was Miss Boxham that had it, but she left when she saw me coming. I wonder what she was after? You don't use a rifle on rabbits."

"Miss Sabina wouldn't demean herself with shooting the rabbits, not with a bow and arrow," Maggie remarked with gentle reproach. "But it's true for you, Mr. Buckle. She got a lend of that gun from the Colonel, the day Mary O'Grady died."

"And do you know why?"

"I do not, Mr. Buckle, not the least little bit in the world.

Miss Sabina never held a gun in her hand since the day she was born. 'Twas Dano saw her leaving the Colonel's house with it, only he wasn't that near to catch what was said."

"But Paddy Fizelle, the boy that sorts Miss Sabina's ridges, found it in the stable there, hidden away behind some tack," Bridie put in. "And he told his a'nt—that's Julia Fizelle —and Julia happened to speak of it at Mary's funeral."

"I see," said Mr. Buckle, although this was far from being the case. It was clear, however, that they had told him now as much as they could and, further, were pining to get back to the *Bugle*. He withdrew, mystified, to puzzle the matter out. Sabina had fired twice, but at whom? The bullet went nowhere near himself. At Barney? Improbable. And why flee like that, when no harm was done and no one was blaming her? Was the episode of the bathroom behind it? He smiled at the recollection, then grew pensive, even rueful. Was he now so odious to her that she could not abide his presence?

At this point the motor launch he had ordered came chugging up to the little pier in his garden and gave a long howl on its klaxon. The speed with which the firm delivered it sprang from the fact that he had paid in advance. Between the slowness of delivery in these parts and the even greater slowness in settling up, there was a connection which had never crossed the local mind. For the next hour or two he was fully occupied in learning how to start, steer and manage the craft; only when he had mastered that and left the engineer back on the mainland did he take the gun again and go after rabbits. He bagged a brace, and to spare the women, drew, skinned and jointed them himself.

There was a grieved expression on Bridie's face as she placed his supper of bacon and eggs before him.

"It was Mother Courage, sir, that got the rabbit," she said. "I'd me back turned only a minute, heating the stewpan, before she'd whipped the lot. Ah, there's the desperate lady! Thanks be to God, you've your little boat and we'll soon be hearing a different story."

"Quiet as a lamb," she reported, back in the kitchen. A reek of burning flesh hung in the air. "A rale gentleman, asked no questions. I'm only disappointed, Miss Sabina would want to shoot him."

"It's on account of him getting the place," said Maggie.

"But where's the sense of a shooting?" Bridie objected. "The place will go to one of his kin that mightn't be as pleasant a lad."

"Then Miss Sabina would up and shoot him too," Maggie asserted. "She's got a lovely mind."

"And be giving us all a bad name!"

"Haven't we that already?" demanded Maggie morosely, with a wave of her hand toward the crumpled *Bugle*. "Are we not shamed in the eyes of the world? What would Mr. Buckle be, only a drop in the ocean?"

"Well, he's paying our wages regular," Bridie remarked. "It's worth preserving him just for that. Mr. Thomas'd only pay when he thought of it, like."

"Still and all . . . Times, I'm lonesome after Mr. Thomas."

"Maybe I am, as well."

Seventeen

AFTER THAT SECOND BULLET, Mr. Barney Roche never stopped running until he reached the haven of Moriarty's. There he made heavy calls on Pio's dwindling supplies and froze the company's blood with an account of his narrow escape from death. Early the next morning, bandaged, plastered, crutch under arm, he limped over to the barracks, to set the wheels of justice in motion. But there were hazards in the case which he had failed to consider, and which Sergeant Foley directly brought to his notice.

"Wait till I tell you, Barney," said that kindly man and sagacious counselor. "It won't be an Inishnamona lad that hears you. He'll be Ballycagey or worse. And he's bound to inquire how your evidence fits with your getting a blind pension."

"What's me pension to do with it? And how's he to know I have one?" Barney expostulated. "Let him only keep to the point."

"They're a terrible nosy lot, justices," the Sergeant replied.

"And with attempted murder in it, he'll probe and probe."

"And what if he does itself? Are you forgetting me da's national record?"

"I am not," said the Sergeant. "But there's another thing, now you've raised it. There's a new kind of justice coming up. They won't bother with national records, only with facts. The grand old spirit is gone. Take my advice, Barney, drop your charge, for the game's not worth the candle."

In urging this on the plaintiff he was not altogether disinterested. If there was one thing he could not abide, it was trouble. He rejoiced in the fact that since he took up his appointment, no one in the district had ever been arrested. There had been one anxious moment when Tacky Dunbar (now dead) was so drunk at the wheel that he charged into the police car, stationary at the barracks door. No arrest was made even then, but Tacky was helped inside and a doctor summoned. To the Sergeant's unbounded relief, that able and experienced practitioner found nothing whatever to suggest an immoderate consumption of liquor. Familiar with Tacky's medical history, he attributed the mishap to a sudden dizzy spell resulting from an operation for mastoid, undergone at the age of fourteen. The relief was great, for apart from all the unpleasantness, there was no accommodation for prisoners: in those happier days, the barracks provided a vital overflow for bed-and-breakfast visitors. It had been touch and go, but common sense prevailed; and from then to the present time, apart from the little matter of the causeway, there had been no other threat to the public peace.

That peace, however, was now in ruins, and the worry was almost too much for the Sergeant to bear.

"Haven't we trouble enough?" he added gloomily, as Barney opened his mouth to reply. "Isn't there plenty round me neck, without your going on?"

For circumstances had arisen compelling the Guards to proceed against no less a figure than Colonel Sentence. He had killed two sheep within eight days of each other, both the property of Tomo O'Shea. He had made no bones about it, had shot them in broad daylight, dragging the carcasses home, skinning and cutting them up and feeding them to the bitches. Major Floud paid for the first, Mrs. Tooth for the second, and the Sergeant hoped that matters would rest at that. But the Colonel struck again. Now it was Larkin's nanny goat that bit the dust, and she in kid, and this time there was a popular outcry. Canon Blender was so unwise as to make a guarded reference to it from the pulpit on the following Sunday, which brought the Colonel to his feet, scarlet with rage.

"Shall Snowdrop and Belle starve in the midst of plenty?" he bawled. "Does a woman stand by with folded hands while her little ones go hungry?"

"Colonel, Colonel, please . . . Kindly resume your seat—"

"If that's your notion of Christianity, I'm off," the Colonel continued, collecting his hat, gloves and stick. "Off for keeps, padre, so now! Come on, me lovelies!" And he swept from his pew and the church with the lovelies capering around him, overjoyed at their sudden release. He made no secret of the fact that his forays would continue as long as the famine lasted, even if Inishnamona were cleared of livestock. Mick Slattery applied for leave to poison his lands and announced it in the *Bugle*; the Colonel gave it out that were this done he would shoot not merely Mick but the chemist supplying the poison. The matter was dropped at once; and on the following day the Colonel slaughtered one of the only two rams on the island.

The Sergeant pleaded with him, cautioned him, appealed to his better self and higher feelings, but all in vain. Major Floud and Mrs. Tooth felt unable to subsidize the brigandage further, and since the Colonel had no money himself, authority was left with no choice. There was nothing for it now but to issue a summons and allow the law to take its dreadful course. And here on top of it all was Barney, blundering about like a bull in a bog!

"The divil fly off with it! Shot like a hound I was, and in open day, going about me lawful occasions, and the Sergeant never turns a hair!" the victim exploded, a single bloodshot eye glaring through his ramshackle bandage. " 'Haven't we trouble enough?' says he. 'Isn't there plenty round me neck?' But as a citizen I'm entitled to satisfaction, and it's how I'm going to get it."

"Who was it put the bandages on you?" queried the Sergeant, suddenly down-to-earth.

"I want the Englishman arrested," Barney went on, brushing the irrelevance aside. "Shooting Christians left and right, like a bloody Black and Tan!"

"We'll see about that. Who was it put the bandages on you?"

There was a pause while Barney made his selection. "Dr. Purcell."

" 'Twas not, then. That's never a doctor's bandage. It's my belief, herself put it on you after your breakfast this morning, just for the walk down here."

This was fighting talk indeed, but the Sergeant was unusually determined. He knew how bitter the feeling already was against Harry Buckle. In their distress and mortification, the people wanted a scapegoat, someone apart from themselves, to blame and punish for their plight—and whom better could they find? Rich, English and of the gentry . . . Mr. Thomas had disappeared without trace, leaving no word. Major Floud was known to suspect foul play. Buckle had shut the great iron gates against them, gates that had stood open all their lives, throughout the Troubles and the Civil War. Their ferry had no sooner sunk than a fine new motorboat appeared at Mount Skellin, and your man was here, there and everywhere, riding the pig's back while the people hungered. Miss Sabina had called him a grabber and borrowed the Colonel's gun. Where was she, what was she doing, that day Dano found her trap in the boreen leading to Norah Fizelle? What had happened to her, that she seemed to take no interest in Inishnamona affairs now? Why did she go round with a pale face and shadows under her eyes? And Bridie and Maggie refused to say a word—were they terrorized, or bought? All the scraps of information the island had were pieced together into a sinister whole, and anything said three times became, in the traditional manner, established and recognized fact. And now Inishnamona's most respected citizen accused the fellow of attempting murder! The storm provoked by the Colonel's misdeeds was but the ruffling of a pond compared to what Sergeant Foley saw a-brewing here.

It was not so much the storm in itself he shrank from as the attitude of his superiors. Nothing came to pass in the island but he knew all about it, but unaccountably, those above seemed to expect him to act as well. They had fairly grilled him after the causeway went up, for instance, although, God help us, what in the world could he do? Send in a secret report denouncing friends and neighbors? Nothing was secret for long in these parts, and a nice time he'd have been given! Now, when the Colonel's case came up, they were likely to start nagging again. Why was the gun not taken away (incidentally, had it a license?), why was no watch kept on the offender's movements, why was he left so long before a summons was issued, why this, why that, why the other—matters clear as day to all familiar with Inishnamona life but beyond the Sergeant's powers of expression when it came to writing an official report.

There's me pension to think of, he reflected, and not so far off, either. And I'm too old to go breaking stones on the building sites of England, like Tim . . .

Barney broke in on this reverie with some fighting talk of his own. "Is it call me a liar?" he shouted. "I'll take it further, then. And I'll be letting them know what class of law and order we're getting here, with men shot down in cold blood and no one raising a finger to help them—no, not were they dying or dead."

"Wisha, Barney," the Sergeant said, unmoved, "amn't I telling you, keep very quiet unless you want another investigation."

"Blackmail!" Barney bellowed. "God bless us, it's blackmail now!" Waving his crutch, he strode vigorously toward the Sergeant as if to chastise him then and there; but the bandage chose this minute to slip down over his face, hanging wreathlike round his neck and exposing his unscathed skull to the public view.

"To be sure," said Sergeant Foley. "To be sure. And there's laying false information, which is an offense, and there's wasting me time, which is a mischief. Anyone else would book you. Go on home now, Barney, and don't be walking the Skellin lands again. And I'm hoping nothing will happen the English boy, for if it does I'll know where to look, and I'm not drawing the blind man's pension either."

With this unchivalrous blow to the body, he brought the interview to a close by the simple method of marching out of the room. Barney had no choice but to retire, frustrated and unappeased. Flinging his crutch into a bog hole, he hastened up to Moriarty's to continue the work of the evening before. There was no stemming the flood. Hours went by and he wasn't talked out until Pio finally closed the bar on the grounds that the day's ration of drink was all used up. This had the curious side effect of winning over to Barney such elements as had not been wholly convinced; and they all trooped off to Målone's in a body, singing, with Barney at their head, to review the position further and lay some plans.

Eighteen

AMONG GOOD IRISH NATIONALISTS, there are two conceptions of the English as a race. According to one, they are the most heartless, ruthless, bloodthirsty ruffians that ever walked the earth. Compared with them, Attila and Genghis Khan were the fine flower of chivalry. The other has it that they are a pitiful, craven, spineless bunch who would hardly dare say boo to a goose. To an outsider, these views might seem to verge on the contradictory, but in fact they are held with profound conviction by the same people at one and the same time.

That second view had been uppermost in Sabina's mind when she borrowed the Colonel's gun. Not for a moment did she propose to kill, wound or even pink Harry Buckle. Her plan was, simply, by firing random shots from time to time in his vicinity, to frighten him away. After a few, a very few, experiences of the sort, he would conclude that the neighborhood was unhealthy and no place for him, and accordingly he would let Thomas know that the deal was off.

The scheme was not so fanciful as it might appear. Sometime before, this technique had proved a resounding success in the case of a German. He was one of the many foreigners bribed by the Government to help Irish industry get on its feet, and he had bought a property on Inishnamona for holidays and weekends. A stream flowed through his land, and in his simple-minded way, he expected to fish the salmon and trout that abounded there. But for some considerable while before he took it, the property had been vacant, and by now the people thought of the fish as a perquisite of their own. The sight of him on the bank with rod and basket, casting and landing in his competent German way, filled them with indignation. They tried at first to make their wishes known by gentle, civilized means: anonymous letters poured through his box, his fences were pulled up and burned, and a few of his windows broken. When this proved unavailing, they had recourse to sterner measures: bullets began to whistle past his ear whenever he walked abroad. Good honest man that he was, he went to the Guards, who were loud in their sympathy, declaring it was scoundrels like that got the country an evil name. But the bullets came whistling by, fast and furious, and although none ever touched him, he finally bowed to the popular will, kept away from the water and eventually ceased to visit the house at all.

If, Sabina had reasoned, a specimen of the martial German race could be routed like this, how much easier it ought to be with a gutless Saxon.

On the day of her first, and last, attempt she had lurked

among the bushes in the garden waiting for him to finish his meal and come out. Seeing the shotgun over his arm when he appeared, she guessed his errand and knew he would make for the dell. More familiar than he with the terrain, she had arrived there a moment or two before he did—though after Barney had shinned up the oak—and took cover behind the rock. She had never pulled a trigger before and she aimed high to make certain the shot went nowhere near, and she was appalled when Barney came tumbling to the ground, as if she had scored a bull's-eye. The men were too far away for their words to be distinguishable, but soon she gathered from their gestures that Barney, unhurt, was accusing Mr. Buckle; and being a decent, fair-minded girl, she fired the second shot to prove him wrong.

The next thing, Barney was making off and Mr. Buckle was calmly walking toward her. He did not even look angry, let alone scared. So far, nothing had gone according to plan, but all had happened so quickly that she felt quite confused; and when she heard him calling her name and bidding her, pleasantly and yet with firmness, to come off it, she lost her head altogether and dashed away.

The position was now that she had suffered a second mortifying defeat at the hands of Mr. Buckle, losing valued equipment in the process. After Snowdrop and Belle, the Colonel's two guns were his most treasured possessions. He had already sent word that he would be glad to have the rifle again, owing to heavy demands on the ammunition used in the shotgun and the difficulty, at present, of replenishing stock. After long, bitter cogitation, Sabina took the only course left open: she wrote stiffly to Mr. Buckle, apologizing for the incident—without stooping, of course, to explain it—and asking him to please return the rifle to its owner. As a correspondent she was hardly more prolific than Thomas himself, and there was not a postage stamp in the house. Rather than entrust the communication to Dano, she harnessed Finn to the trap and drove with it to the post office.

It was a Friday morning, and the small office was crowded with old men drawing their pensions, all from England, and women their family allowances. Sabina waited her turn as the piles of notes changed hands, observing the grin on Teresa Larkin's chops as she drew for her three young children, as yet unborn. Sabina had heard tales of such doings but had never before actually witnessed them: the squalor of it, the satisfied faces, the greedy hands were painful to watch.

"Not that there's a whole lot you could buy," remarked Teresa, counting her money and putting it away with an important look. "There isn't a pot of jam in the place."

"And the youngsters look for jam, eh, Teresa?" someone put in, with a chuckle. A roar of laughter greeted this sally, in which Delia, the postmistress, wholeheartedly joined.

"Ah, you couldn't blame her, the creature," Delia said when at length she and Sabina were alone. "Sure, what harm? The country will never miss it."

"It's a fraud, all the same," was the cool rejoinder.

"Of course, a lady like yourself has her own way of looking at it," Delia said. She was so anxious to agree with everyone that it was hard to know what opinions, if any, she really held. "But poor Teresa, now. She could claim for five, if the fancy took her. She's married long enough."

Having thus paid tribute to Mrs. Larkin's discretion, she

inquired what might be done for Miss Boxham. "Oh, God, is it ninepenny stamps?" she cried in dismay. "I haven't one, nor threepennies, nor sixpennies neither. Indeed, there's nothing left but the two and nines for America. Would that be of any interest at all? There's a picture of Dan O'Connell on them, he's gorgeous."

"I certainly shall not put two and nine on a letter down the road," Miss Boxham stated flatly. "Ninepence is wicked enough. Do you realize our postal rates are the third highest in Europe?"

"I do! It was on the paper," Delia said complacently. "Ah, they can't beat us. I'd say, we'll go higher yet. But what'll you do? Dan's gone or he'd maybe smuggle it over. Can you wait till the scholars are home and I'll send one across? The scholars are better than any postman."

Sabina agreed to the enlistment of a schoolchild, left her ninepence for him and turned to go. But she was not to escape so lightly: to keep her there, if only for a few moments longer, Delia hurriedly asked, "And did you hear from Mr. Thomas since?" No one knew better than she who heard from whom.

"I did not," Sabina replied brusquely, as the point was a sore one. "My brother seldom writes letters."

"Mr. Buckle had nothing, too," the postmistress divulged with a sigh. "He was telling me so the other day," she added quickly. "Ah well, I suppose there's enough to see and do in London without the confusion of correspondence. There'll be all the more to say to you when he's home again."

Sabina refused to be drawn and left the office. Outside, Julia Fizelle, Bridget Foley and Mary Malone patiently waited, in the hope of getting a lift. The usual method of travel on Inishnamona was to hail a passing vehicle, and at the journey's end, give the driver the price of a drink, but with the disappearance of cars, tractors and traveling shops from the road, people now had to walk or stay at home. Sabina's neighbors had already covered the seven miles, hot and dusty, from village to post office and she could not bring herself to disappoint them; but her heart bled for Finn, who flinched and tossed his mane as one after the other the three large ladies mounted the step and sank heavily onto the cushioned seat. By the time he had dragged them home, his flanks were heaving and his coat was dark with sweat. Sabina resolved to saddle and ride him in the future and leave the neighbors to shift for themselves.

She took the aggrieved cob out of the shafts and turned him loose in the field. The yellow flags by the marshy border were crumpled and wilting for want of rain. Traces of scarlet showed here and there in the fuchsia hedge, a month before their time. The beans and peas that Buckle had planted for her were sallow and withered. Either you were drenched for weeks on end in this bediviled region, or else you were parched with drought. Not the least little feather of cloud appeared in the sky. Across the water, the blue mountains stretched away mile after mile into the distance, beautiful as a dream, in the pearly haze that promised more hot weather.

A motor launch shot round the bend, leaping through the placid sea, shoveling the water aside in its haste. As it drew nearer she recognized the man at the wheel as Harry Buckle, who was frowning sternly as if much annoyed. With him were two strangers, sitting bolt upright in the stern, grim, wooden-faced, staring before them without a word. They were not from Inishnamona, that was certain—there was an unmistakable Inish-namona face, thanks to generations of intermarrying, and neither of them had it—and anyhow, she knew all the local men, by sight if nothing more. But it was equally certain that they had business of some sort with her, for Buckle was steering hard for the slip-way below her cottage. As she watched them, she divined what that business was and her heart missed a beat.

These were plain-clothes men from Ballycagey. Buckle had reported the incident in the dell. It was the kind of despicable act to which his nation was prone. Under the pretext of performing a civic duty or upholding the law, or some other pitiful nonsense, they were always prepared to denounce, persecute and ruin the harmless and honest. Not content with all else he had done, Buckle had now resolved to see her in prison. There was no rancor worse than that of villains for those they have injured. Well! If he expected her to cringe and whine before him, he was in for a disappointment. Like the martyrs of history, she would deny nothing, explain nothing, plead for nothing. Head high, she moved to the top of the slipway and stood there, proudly waiting, defying them to do their worst.

But as the launch drew up alongside, a remarkable change occurred in all the occupants. The frown on Buckle's face disappeared and was replaced by a beaming smile, while the rigid looks of the others gave way to lubberly grins of relief at reaching dry land. Nor, as Buckle hailed her, did he speak with the voice of a man about to prefer charges.

"May we come ashore?" he asked gaily, as if at their last meeting they had parted the warmest of friends.

"Certainly, if you wish," Miss Boxham replied with queenly

composure. "But mind yourself on the seaweed," she could not help adding.

Buckle climbed over the side of the launch and came gingerly up the slipway to greet her. "We did it in seven minutes," he said with pride, glancing at his watch. "Not bad for a maiden voyage. And it's the first time I ever put to sea. Viking blood, I presume." From his easy manner of talking, the episodes in the bathroom and the dell might never have taken place.

"My passengers were never at sea before, either," he went on. "They were a little dubious about it in the beginning, but when I said it was for a lady they agreed at once, stout fellows that they are. If you'll excuse me, I'll just help unload."

"But who are these men?" Sabina asked. They, too, were disembarking, one with a heavy bag of tools. "And what are they doing here?"

"They are plumbers from Ballycagey," was the reply, "and they are going to put your bath in. This launch only came yesterday evening or I would have done about it sooner. I hope, by the way, that this is a convenient time? It was now or wait until Monday."

Sabina's emotions were unusually mixed, even for her. Uppermost was a surge of joy at the news, but she also deplored the loss of a grievance, mourned her hopes of martyrdom and resented the actions of Mr. Buckle. He behaves like a landlord, she reflected crossly, but aloud she could only mumble, "There's no cement."

But Buckle had brought cement, and much more besides: meat, fish, fruit, vegetables, butter, bread, all fresh and appetizing, such as no longer were to be found on Inishnamona.

"Why have you done all this?" Sabina demanded somewhat indistinctly, as her mouth was watering.

"It's a bribe," he told her without hesitation.

"I thought as much!"

"Yes—I'm hoping you'll give me a cup of coffee. Now, you show our friends—by the way, they're Sam and Joe—to the bathroom like a dear thing and I'll take these things to the kitchen."

Sabina was about to remark that she was not a dear thing, but decided against it. In Mr. Buckle's presence she was forever sounding childish or looking foolish, she could not imagine why: her best plan seemed to be to maintain a dignified silence. She conducted the plumbers to the bathroom and left them there, gazing aghast at Shamus' work; then she went to the kitchen, filled a kettle, put it on and started grinding the coffee.

"Soon there won't be any water," she observed with gloomy satisfaction.

"Then you must come to the house," he said. "By the way, please don't imagine I brought the plumbers here on . . . on account of . . . I mean, I do want you still to look on the house as yours and to make every use of it."

"You won't have any water, either," she replied, implacable.

"But we are on the main supply," he pointed out.

"That means nothing out here. Except that you pay the rates."

"Oh."

There was a pause while Buckle digested this information. Sabina looked at the provisions that he had deposited on the table, noting among them a brand of creamery butter as a rule reserved for export or the smarter shops in Dublin: it took a

Buckle, she reflected with mortification, to run it to earth in Ballycagey.

"There's a letter on the way to you," she said, embarrassed. "I didn't expect to see you, and so I wrote."

"Give me the gist of it, then," he said, smiling, "and I will tear it up unread."

Diabolical how he always took the point.

"It wasn't anything much," she said, coloring up. "Only, I was sorry if I startled you. And would you kindly return that gun to Colonel Sentence soon? He really is odd. He seemed quite willing to lend it and then almost at once he asked for it back. Said the ammunition for his other one was getting low."

"I'm not surprised to hear it," Buckle said with a joyous peal of laughter.

He was much surprised, however, to find that she knew nothing of the Colonel's exploits. Inishnamona rang with them, yet not a whisper had reached her ears. But even stranger than her ignorance of current affairs was her reaction as he revealed them to her now. She was neither astonished, amused nor concerned, but simply and unaccountably looked wretched, gazing at him in silence with the eyes of a wounded child.

"It's all right, you know." he said, restraining his mirth. "They won't behead him. We'll sort it out between us, and Snowdrop and Belle will get their rations, now that we have the launch. And I'll shoot round with the rifle as soon as I've had a bit more practice. It's one thing coming up the Sound, another braving the open Atlantic. And I can't go by car because of the gates. They won't open."

"Why did you shut them?"

"Just out of curiosity, to see if I could."

"Oh." There was another pause. "We thought you wanted to keep us out," she volunteered then, in a small voice, blushing again.

"I thought only the Pope, royalty and nursemaids said 'We' and 'Us' when they meant 'I' and 'me,' " Buckle observed. "Now listen, Sabina, once and for all. You are extremely naughty. I don't deserve this. I have done nothing to you whatsoever. Thomas chooses to sell his house to me. I beg you to look on it, always, as your own. Would that happen if he sold it to someone else? To nuns or hotelkeepers, as I suggested the other day that he might?"

It was true that the suggestion had been made, but as so often happens, Sabina had thought of a good reply to it since.

"But you see, he wouldn't, he's far too lazy," she said. "He would never exert himself to look for a buyer or advertise. It had to be someone on the spot, like you. Someone determined, unscrupulous and wily!" she concluded, tossing her head.

"You don't know as much about your brother as you imagine," said Buckle gravely. "You have no idea how many people come up to the house to ask for him, all wanting advice or help in some matter. And you've no idea how able he is. What you call laziness is merely paralysis. He needs scope of a nature he can't find here, and he's gone to look for it."

"In England!" said Sabina with a bitter laugh. "Well, perhaps I don't know my own brother, nor value him as I should, but I'll tell you one thing: he won't stand a hellhole like that for long."

"I bow to your superior knowledge, both of your brother

and of my country," said Buckle, his bland and genial self again. "Now, I'm not going to scold any more. Isn't that water rather a time in boiling?"

"There's no use trying to hurry us here in Ireland," Sabina replied, complacently putting a hand to the kettle. "It's not heating at all!" she cried. She ran to the electric light switch and turned it on, with no result. "The current's off again!" she exploded. "It's more often off than on."

"Do you think the plumbers turned it off while they do the work?"

"No, I don't. They had no need to. The immersion heater is the one thing in the cottage that never gave trouble, and the wiring was mended just the other week. I saw it done. No, it's Inishnamona. If it isn't the current it's the telephone or the pump or the chimney. And soon there'll be a drought." She sank into a chair and buried her face in her hands. "You little know what you're up against," came in a muffled tone. "Just you wait and see."

As if to lend force to her words, at this moment there came a resounding crash, followed by a cloud of dust which made it impossible even to guess what happened. When this had cleared somewhat, they glimpsed a yawning aperture in the kitchen wall, its jagged rim framing the startled faces of Sam and Joe, who both began to talk at once. The mammoth immersion heater, Sabina's comfort and joy, was riveted to a board which in turn was cemented into the wall dividing the bathroom and kitchen, and now, weakened by Shamus' frenetic and random blows, the structure had given way, pitching the heater forward into the bath.

"Thank God you were not inside it, ma'am," said Joe devoutly.

"Or else you were squashed like a beetle," his mate chimed in.

It was the last straw, the crowning humiliation. Sabina broke into helpless tears. "Oh, damn Ireland!" she sobbed. "Damn Ireland!"

"Dear Sabina, please don't," cried Buckle in deep distress and much bewilderment. To his free, happy English mind, the disaster was merely something to deal with and put to rights; that to her it might be a symbol of national failure, causing her to writhe in personal shame, was beyond his understanding. "What on earth does it matter?"

"It would happen when you were there," she wailed.

"What odds?" She was not an easy girl to understand. "Just as well we were here. It might have fallen in on you, as Joe says."

"I only wish it had."

"Come, come, come. You can put it up again, can't you, boys?"

"We can, of course," they said at once. "Only for the plastering, till the ciment dries out."

"And Peadar's gone to England!" But she recovered herself so far as to invite Mr. Buckle to the sitting room and give him a glass of sherry.

He chatted with her pleasantly while the men were working, which they did with a will, as invariably their kind does in time of trouble. She grew steadily more despondent; by the time the job was done and the three men had left, she was about ready to cut her throat. Everything began to weigh on her mind at once.

Why had no one, not Julia, not Dano, not a soul she came across, breathed a word about the Colonel and his pranks? Clearly because she no longer mattered, was no longer Miss Boxham of Mount Skellin. Unaware of the dark stirrings in the local mind, the first result of which, as ever, was the ending of communication with the gentry, she could find no other explanation. And the change in status had brought home a terrible truth to herself. It was as Miss Boxham of Mount Skellin that she had identified with the island people, fought their battles, defended their cause. Now the bottom had fallen out of her world, the game was up, and she didn't give a tinker's damn. And on top of that, it was apparently her lazy, selfish, subversive brother that everyone liked and trusted, and—here her tears began to flow again—she missed him, awful as he was, like blazes too.

The telephone rang: it was the postmistress.

"Is Mr. Buckle with you there?" she asked, well knowing that he was not. As if the launch could have passed by her window without her spotting it! "Because a telegram's after coming for him."

"Well, he's gone," Sabina said between her sniffles.

"It's from Mr. Thomas," Delia said. "Will I read it to you? I shouldn't, of course, only it looks like there's a mistake in it and you could maybe sort it—"

"What mistake? What d'you mean?" Sabina broke in abruptly, while her heart began to pound.

"There's only two words in it at all. Now, would it be 'Sold everything' or 'Told everything'? Which would you be inclined to favor?"

"Which does it say?" Sabina all but screamed.

"Neither one. That's what has me bet. It says: 'Hold every-thing." But that doesn't make sense, does it now?"

Profound heavenly peace invaded Sabina's mind.

"It makes all the sense in the world," she said, and put the receiver back.

Nineteen

THE BALLYCAGEY *Bugle* persisted in looking to Inishnamona for lead stories and editorial comment. There was no malice in this, no deliberate hounding or systematic persecution. It was simply that the island doings made a welcome change from the wrangles of the local council, the charges of drunken disorder, the suspected cases of fowl pest, and the bursts of the bishop on this or that, which normally filled its pages.

The people smarted under it, nevertheless. For one thing, thanks to the drought, for the first time in memory they were able to read it from cover to cover. Before Inishnamona became an island, deliveries had been made by the bus, from which a bundle of copies was tossed out on the road at various points; afterward the papers were all thrown down together at the ferry landing. In either case they lay until collected, quietly soaking up the puddles until large areas of reading matter were undecipherable. Now—apart from a few rents and smears, a page or so missing where the newsagent required it for wrapping, an odd passage obscured where he had done some arithmetic—the full text was open to their inspection.

The latest windfall to come the *Bugle*'s way was the trial of Colonel Sentence. Owing to delays in the postal service, due to the loss of the ferry, the sergeant had confided the details to the courthouse in Ballycagey by telephone, and the telephone on that occasion was in one of its moods. The Sergeant heard, clear as a whistle, the voice of the man at the other end—"Right you be, Sarge . . . I've got that, Sarge . . . Leave the rest to me, Sarge"— and he assumed that his own was equally plain. In fact, it went over as a faint gurgle, and the framing of the indictment was wholly different from what he had expected. Mrs. Tooth and Major Floud, whom he had asked to attend as witnesses for the Colonel and who had willingly agreed, intending to pay whatever fine was imposed, found themselves joined with him as defendants. As the summonses were served in the Irish tongue, neither had the least idea of what was in store, and were much surprised at being shepherded into the dock, together with the accused and his bitches.

The kindly Sergeant hastened across and muttered under his breath, " 'Twill be all right, ma'am. Don't mind them, Major. A technical hitch, but we'll get it sorted." He had come to the conclusion, and the clerk of the court agreed, that as the pair of them proposed to face the music anyhow, the best way out was to let things take their course.

But what made the *Bugle*'s day and bore fruit beyond anything that might have been anticipated, was the evidence of the Colonel himself. Harry Buckle had kept his promise, and supplies of meat, bones, biscuits and vitamin E had arrived for Snow-drop and Belle. The Colonel deemed the shootings to be things of the past, and whether in the dock or, as his privilege was, in the box, declined to discuss them. Instead, he fulminated against the dilatory ways of your men in Dublin. He had informed those men of priceless natural resources hidden in the soil of Inish-namona. They had appeared to take a proper and lively interest: experts had been sent who made exhaustive researches lasting a fortnight, but from that day on, not another single step had been taken.

"Will one of you give the lady a chair," the Justice broke in, when this had been under way for some time. Mrs. Tooth was accommodated, and the Colonel resumed his address.

Until that morning he had mentioned the matter to only three others. He was at any time a man of few words—here the Justice stopped taking notes and stared at him in a daze—and this was something better kept dark. But now the time had come to speak out. Part, at least, of the natural resources referred to lay in his lands, and it was as plain as the nose on your face that Dublin was conspiring to cheat him of his rights. That, and only that, could explain their silence—

"Who are the three other persons in question?" the Justice inquired, more in the hope of staunching the flow than from real curiosity.

"Tom, Sabby and Buckle."

"Who are Tom, Sabby and Buckle?" his Honor persisted. "Are they in court?"

The Sergeant described Tom, Sabby and Buckle, adding that

none was present and Mr. Boxham's whereabouts even unknown.

"It doesn't matter," the Justice said pettishly. "How did we get on this at all? I'm hearing about the malicious slaughter of livestock, amn't I? And I find it proven," he shouted as the Colonel opened his mouth to continue. "Return to the dock please, prisoner, till I give judgment."

With the dignity of a samurai condemned by his lord to *seppuku*, the Colonel strode back to the dock, while Snowdrop and Belle frisked happily round him. The Justice's decisions were strange, but like everything strange in Irish affairs, not without ample precedent. Major Floud was fined fifty pounds, ordered to compensate in full and pay all costs; Mrs. Tooth was bound, in the sum of twenty-five pounds, to be of good behavior for twelve months and a day; and the charges against the Colonel were dropped. The Major's cries for mercy were drowned by an excited hum in the well of the courtroom.

"I had to stop the fellow's gob, if the ceiling itself fell in," the Justice later remarked, over his luncheon, to the prosecuting attorney. "Did you see the press boys writing away? Next thing, there'd be an inquiry, God help us, and we don't want that."

Here he spoke not for himself alone but for practically everyone engaged in public life. Colonel Sentence was plainly a nut, his talk of natural resources cock-and-bull, but equally it was plain that a pair of civil servants, using him as a pretext, had spent a fortnight on Inishnamona, having the time of Riley at the expense of the Irish taxpayer.

None of this, in the capable hands of the *Bugle*, was lost in the telling. And as always occurs in summarized reporting, various remarks that were simple enough in themselves made, when dragged from their context, an impression far more sinister than circumstances warranted. The Sergeant's reply to the Justice—"Tom and Sabby, your Honor, are Mr. Thomas and Miss Sabina Boxham, formerly of Mount Skellin. Mr. Buckle is an English gentleman who has bought the place from Mr. Boxham. They are none of them here today. Mr. Boxham has left the country, and his address is unknown—" was, by a caprice of the printer, set in heavier type than the rest of the story, but even without this accidental emphasis, in the present emotional state of the island it would have caused an upheaval.

Now everything fell into place. It had been like a jigsaw puzzle, a confused jumble of fragments with just a few more vividly colored and distinctively shaped than the rest which, once pieced together, led to the solution of the whole. These outstanding items were Harry Buckle, Sabina's cry of "Grabber!" and her borrowing of the gun, the disappearance of Thomas and the two mysterious visitors to the island. Whatever the natural resources were that the Colonel knew of, Buckle knew of them too: therefore he was out to seize them for himself. For what other reason would a rich man settle there, only to get richer still? The funnel and masts of the ferry, sticking up when the tide was low, slid into the picture too. Buckle it was who had planned and executed the wreck, the better to carry out his schemes in the isolation that followed. That launch of his must have been ordered months or years ahead; nothing, on Inishnamona, had ever yet been supplied in a couple of weeks. The big iron gates had been closed as a warning to the inquisitive to keep away. The attempt on Barney's life was made with a similar purpose.

All fitted in to perfection, more or less. It was true that certain facts refused to march in line. For instance, the ferry had given cause for alarm long before Buckle ever appeared on the scene. And he was known to have brought Mr. Thomas to town for the train that morning and to have left him there, safe and sound. Further, there was the telegram from Mr. Thomas himself within the last few days, incomprehensible though it was. And never mind what Miss Sabina said to Buckle, he had brought plumbers out from the mainland to fix her bath; and it was he, not she, who returned the rifle to Colonel Sentence, the sort of thing a friend would do. And then there was the fellow himself, so quiet and pleasant, busy from morning to dusk, weeding, hoeing, trimming, planting, when he wasn't acting as unpaid ferry. Either he was innocent as a babe or, as Father Kelly remarked, he was the most consumptive actor alive.

But the anti-Buckle party would have none of this. Magnificently, they rose above it. To do so was essential to their happiness and peace of mind. Nailing him as the villain was like coming home after a sojourn in fearsome places, to a pattern of things they understood and where they knew the moves. The cruel Saxon, the eternal foe, threatened them once again, and they would best him. Again they applied to their friends beyond for advice and assistance. The forces of British imperialism in the North had recently been augmented, under a new commander known to be tough as a boot, and this had produced a lull in the fight for justice and freedom, leaving the crusaders with time on their hands. Grim shaggy individuals quietly came and went: none but the chosen knew their business or dared to ask it; and the Sergeant sighed and scratched his head and dismally awaited the outcome.

Twenty

SPRAWLED IN A DECK CHAIR, Buckle rested from his labors, sipping sherry and gazing out to sea. Every now and again a gull fell upon the water, *smack*, as if shot, seized the fish it had noted from on high and flew off with it. Otherwise not a ripple appeared on the surface, which mirrored the colors of the evening, a predominance of gold and silver touched here and there with faint rose or lilac: exquisite effects heralding the break of the long fine spell and the approach of ugly weather.

This, Buckle did not know. He thought only he had never seen the place more lovely, and he was more than usually carefree and content. The day had passed in ideal fashion. In the morning he had come on a magnificent mulberry tree, neglected and forlorn, emancipated it from stifling hangers-on, cleared space around for sun and light. After lunch, for all the lucid air, he caught his first trout, a couple of them, not far from the boulder whence the shots had been fired. Then back to work, removing two cartwheels and a bedstead from gaps in a fence and replacing them with stakes and wire, less traditional but more effective.

The job was barely done before he received his first caller: the first, that is, who had actually come to see him and not to inquire for Thomas. Few things aroused in Colonel Sentence any feelings of warmth for his fellow-men, but kindness to Snowdrop and Belle was one. The way this fellow had fetched their grub in his launch and braved the rocky coast to bring it round had won his heart; he did not, for once, even suspect an ulterior motive. And since no gentleman accepts a service without making such return as may lie in his power, with his last two cartridges he dispatched a couple of ducks, the property of Michael Malone, and wearing his good suit, now arrived at Mount Skellin to make the presentation.

"So you've heard from young Tom," he remarked when compliments and thanks were at an end. "A telegram, I gather."

"A telegram? No indeed."

The procedure with telegrams on Inishamona was this: except in the rare case of recipients with a telephone, they were treated as ordinary mail. Dano delivered them with the other letters on the following day. The delay was of no importance, as anything urgent was confided to post office customers or passers-by and went round the island at kingfisher speed. After her talk with Sabina, Delia had duly rung Mount Skellin, but without result, and she had therefore handed the written message, on the official form and in the official envelope, to Dano when he collected the post in the morning. This was the normal routine, but as far as Mount Skellin was concerned, the normal routine was in abeyance. Dano was even more incensed by the shutting of the gates than the people at large, as it resulted in extra work for himself: he must either drag his bicycle over the steep grassy bank beside them or leave it on the road and walk for a good quarter mile. He tried first one and then the other, and then hit on another solution altogether. Just within the gates stood a partly hollowed tree, and into this he took to stuffing Mr. Buckle's mail. It was his intention to bring this practice into line with official requirements by carving the words *Mount Skellin Post Box* into the bark, but he could never remember to bring a knife. Here, then, reposed the telegram from Thomas, together with much else, both in the way of correspondence and of leaves, feathers, eggshells, insects and a nest of squirrels.

"Well, there was one," the Colonel said. "I suppose you'll see it the week after next, if ever. We probably get just the skim off what people send." Here he was struck by a sudden thought, and the mad glare kindled in his eyes. "I say, though! Makes you think. What if those lads in Dublin were writing me all this time, and certain forces took care the letters never reached me? Hey?"

Buckle made haste to reply; he presumed it was on the cards.

"It's as well, then, I spoke out as I did the other day," the Colonel remarked with complacence. "And I take off my hat to the *Bugle*. Printed the lot verbatim. The press at its best. Serious matters given priority, and no damn knockabout farce."

Buckle again concurred, although quite at sea as to what the Colonel could mean. Then, excusing himself, he carried the ducks to the kitchen, requested Maggie to roast one for dinner, and returned to his guest with a tray of drinks. The Colonel was on the prowl through the drawing room, shaking the massive curtains, pulling sofas and chairs from their wonted places and peering behind screens.

"The girls are on edge," he said by way of explanation, and in fact Snowdrop and Belle were running up and down with little whinges of apprehension or pointing, ears cocked, paw up, head to one side, rigid as fireside ornaments.

"Perhaps the house is strange to them."

"They know the house like the back of my hand. No, there's something here they don't like!" said the Colonel, delving into the late Mrs. Boxham's work basket with the air of a man not easily fooled.

"Then let us have our drinks outside. It's a beautiful day, and they will be happier in the garden."

"All the same, I should check your security," the Colonel said, reluctantly closing the basket again and following his host. "Always be prepared. Canon Blender came to the house today without prior arrangement, and fell into one of my tank traps. Now d'ye see the point? If you don't take trouble, you don't get results. Thanks, whiskey for me."

They drank and chatted together pleasantly. Now and again the bitches went bounding off, barking hysterically, but nothing came of it, no cries of fear or pain, and soon they trotted back to lie at their master's feet. For his part, under the influence of the spirit, he quickly grew talkative and sentimental.

"Sabby, now there's a dear thing. And she was saying some very jolly things about you," he revealed at one point.

"Oh, when was that? It is only a few days since she loosed off a couple of bullets in my direction."

"And muffed them both?" The Colonel smiled with fatherly toleration. "We must walk before we can run. Though beginner's luck is a curious thing, y'know. First time I ever fired a loaded rifle (Sandhurst, 1913 class), I bagged the instructor. But what are we talking about? Ah, to be sure—Sabby. No, it was just today she was cracking you up. Just now. She ran me over here like the decent girl she is, and she's down at the gates, waiting to bring me home."

"But why? Why doesn't she come in?"

"How can she, when the gates are closed? I had the deuce of a time heaving myself over the bank, I can tell you. And she wouldn't leave Finn after her, tied up and alone. Ah, she's a great girl. Yes, she fairly cried you up, and yet it came out queerly too, as if you were dead. How shall I put it?" The Colonel racked his brain for an image and found what he sought. "In the war—the first war, the real war—I used to go out on recce alone, early, behind the enemy lines. For a bit of a lark and to get up an appetite for breakfast. I'd see a Boche, one particular Boche that I'd choose to hate more than the rest, and I'd creep upon him with never a thought in my skull but how to do him in. And when it was over, and he was lying there on the ground, quiet and still, I got the oddest feeling about him, all chummy and gentle and somehow admiring. We could do with more of that in the world today," the Colonel strongly asserted here, branching off, but re-collecting himself, he soon continued. "Yes, I reckon that's how Sabby feels about you, even though the bullets went wide. You may not be dead, but you're no longer the enemy. See what I mean?"

"Not entirely. I don't quite grasp the analogy, that is. Why should Miss Boxham have regarded me as an enemy?" For the innocent Buckle believed such matters were hid from all but themselves.

"How do I know? But Sabby borrows me rifle, you bring it back, in the meantime she's fired on you twice. Piecing it all together, I get the impression she had something against you. And that the something is now removed."

"But I'm afraid it's not," Buckle said with a sigh.

"Well, to hear her talking, you're the cat's whiskers. Or the deceased cat's whiskers, shall we say?"

The Colonel had never been known to smile at another man's joke, yet none was more appreciative of the few he made himself. He roared, coughed and spluttered now until the bitches looked up in alarm and disapproval. Then, pulling himself together at last, he declared that Sabby would think he was dead, and with a final word of thanks on behalf of Snowdrop and Belle he went away with them, weaving over the grass and into the long, dark, leafy tunnel. Buckle was left alone, to contemplation and his sherry.

It did not take him long to explain away the Colonel's remarks about Sabina: she had finally been won over by his efforts in the matter of her bathtub, and wished for the war to end. Her praises had been uttered expressly for the Colonel to pass on; it was her proud method of asking for truce. It struck him, nevertheless, that the letter she spoke of having written and which he had promised to destroy unread, had not reached him, and this in turn brought up the question of her brother's telegram. No doubt in the confusion prevailing all over the island both had been lost. Sometime tomorrow he must ask for a copy of that wire, bound to be Thomas' London address, belated but welcome.

The rosy lights were fading, leaving just a shimmer of silvery gold. Practical thoughts drifted easily to the back of his mind. With every minute that passed, his sense of well-being grew. Here was life, and he had found it, stumbled on it by chance. This was life: rescuing old mulberry trees, fishing for trout, mending fences, digging, hoeing, scything, making hay. He felt, as he had never felt about any meal before, that he had earned the roasting duck in the oven, earned it truly in a way unknown to businessmen and factory hands.

A poem he had learned in childhood, buried for years, came to him all at once: "Where the quiet-colored end of evening smiles/miles on miles/on the solitary pastures where our sheep/half asleep/tinkle homeward . . . How did it go on? Start again. "Where the quiet-colored end of evening smiles," Buckle recommenced aloud, his forehead puckered in concentration, "miles on miles . . ."

A familiar cutting sardonic voice broke in.

"Never mind the quiet-colored end of evening," Thomas snarled. "Just give me a slug of that whiskey before I croak!"

Harry Buckle was used to the foibles of his friend. Before Thomas came to the reasons for this unexpected arrival, there would first have to be a string of complaints about the journey. On the Day of Judgment itself, thought Harry, Tom was sure to hold things up with a tirade about the trouble of finding the court and the inconvenience of the hour fixed for the hearing. Therefore he passed him a generous noggin without a word and waited in patience for what would follow.

It was to be conceded that even by local standards, Thomas' journey had not been ordinary. He had flown across the evening before and caught the night mail to Ballycagey, meaning to continue by road; since passengers used this train almost never, a fleet of buses waited for it to bring them to their various destinations. But on this occasion the train was packed with men back from England for their summer holiday. And that afternoon Ireland had beaten the Solomon Islands at table tennis; in the wild celebrations of the capital the holidaymakers had missed their usual train. On reaching Ballycagey around six in the morning they were still in a festive mood and stopped the bus at every pub, coaxing or threatening the sleepy landlord until he let them in, and bringing the driver as well, for fear of defection. After a while they left the route and broke new country; shortly after that, the driver passed out and a passenger took his place. The trip lasted three and a half times as long as it ought to, indeed only came to an end as the sun was sinking. The shore of the mainland was littered with sleeping bodies, the bus was over its hood in water, no vessel was in sight and Thomas had been forced to pick his way over the jagged rocks of the causeway. He was starving, cold, wet, cut, bruised, unshaven, and above all this, he yearned to shoot one in ten of the Irish people.

"But, my dear fellow, why not let me know you were coming?"

"How could I, without letting everyone else know as well? And after all that has happened, I want a day or two of peace. So not a word to a soul—and now, for God's sake, give me something to eat."

Buckle obediently hurried indoors, Thomas following at his leisure. At the top of the granite steps he paused to scowl at the all-too-familiar sweep of the country around. What on earth should he say to Harry, how explain that the deal was off? That the whole idea had been madness, that he could as soon escape his lot as a hunchback his, that there was no room in his mind, really none, for anything but the land of his birth, on which he so tirelessly heaped his invectives? He had seen it all happen so many times before. Old Roger Sentence was exactly the same. You loathed the very thought of Ireland, yet you could live no-where else, no other place would do. You might flee to the end of the earth, something always dragged you back . . .

But now Harry came trotting up, looking bewildered, carrying a plate of bread and cheese.

"You'd better eat this while you wait," he said. "I am awfully sorry, but something odd has happened. An hour ago and more I gave Maggie a duckling to roast for supper, and it ought to be just about ready. And there it is on the table where I left it, not even plucked. And both the women have cleared out and taken their belongings away. Their potted plants have gone, and so has the Infant of Prague. What d'you think it can mean?"

Thomas fell on the bread and cheese and consumed it before he replied. "I have no idea," he said then. "I would imagine that it is meaningless."

"But they have never done such a thing before. They have been as good as gold. And they can't intend to come back, or why remove their possessions?"

"Something must have upset them. These people live on their vanity." Thomas was beginning to feel at home. "The most probable answer is, they didn't know how to roast a bird and left in a huff.

"But do you mean to tell me," he cried in the next breath, "that I'm to wait until you have plucked and roasted it yourself?"

Harry hastened to calm this fear. There were, he said, two fine plump trout, each weighing about two and a half pounds, caught that very afternoon, which should be fried at once. "Unless, of course, Mother Courage—"

At the mention of that name, Thomas flew to the kitchen without another word, but for once the delinquent cat was blameless, in fact nowhere to be seen. The trout lay on a dish in the pantry, next to an uncovered bowl of cream, all untouched. The ducklings were on the kitchen table, their eyes half closed, their feathers stained with blood. Yet nothing barred the way to these dainties: every single door, inner and outer, was standing open. Mother Courage had simply vanished, along with the potted plants and the Infant of Prague.

Strange as it all was, both young men had other things on their minds for the present. Harry busied himself preparing the meal while Thomas sat looking on and abusing London. There was nothing to be said for it whatsoever, or for anyone resident there. Not merely were the English feckless, cunning, lazy, smelly and rude, but to crown it all, there were next to none of them left. You'd walk the streets by the hour and never hear English spoken, not even in the grisly accents of the BBC. And just listen to this! Once he went into a teashop and ordered tea with bread and butter, and the waiter brought him coffee and Melba toast. And do you know why? The fellow was fresh from Istanbul. The manager backed him to the hilt. Said the modern way to order was to point to a number on the menu, not by confusing the staff with a foreign language.

"Foreign language!" Thomas stormed. "In Knightsbridge. *Within a stone's throw of Harrod's.*" And something not dissimilar had taken place in London Airport itself.

But then Harry put the fish on the table and opened a bottle of wine, and Thomas allowed the subject to drop. At supper they chatted vaguely of local doings: the sinking of the ferry, the imminence of famine, the trial of Colonel Sentence and its bizarre result. Dusk had fallen, a dim ghostly twilight from which all trace of color had seeped away, with only the dark shapes of trees and bushes visible through it. From somewhere near among those trees there came a cry: *To-whit to-whit to-woo!* Harry broke off sharply in the middle of a sentence, listening. Softly from farther off came an answering hoot. On his feet in a moment, he ran to the open door and stood there, listening intently again, while Thomas looked on, amused.

"What's up? Did you never hear an owl before?"

"Ssshhh!"

Once more came the nearby hoot, once more the far-off, faint reply. Harry slowly walked back to the table and sat down, looking thoughtful.

"Yes, I've heard an owl before," he said, "but never a hermaphrodite owl. You see, the male calls *tu-whit tu-whit!* and any female interested replies *to-woo!* These owls are uttering both the cries at once. An ornithologist like myself is bound to be a little curious, especially as the nearer bird, at least, calls in a strong but charming brogue. Just wait and see . . ."

Obligingly, a moment or two later, the calls were repeated.

"Well, to be sure! You're pretty wide-awake," smiled Thomas. "And trust them to make a hames somewhere. Think no more of it, however. If you are going to tease your powerful brain with every little bit of childish nonsense the locals get up to—"

He was interrupted at this point by a tremendous bang

which shook the old house from top to bottom and went echoing round the sky. It was followed by noises suggesting a severe hailstorm, shouts, apparently of approval, the barking of many dogs and an outcry from every ass in the vicinity. For a moment or so the two young men stared at each other; then they leaped up, tore out of the kitchen, and guided by the symphony of brays, barks and voices, sprinted down the drive toward the iron gates.

Twenty-one

THE EVENTS OF THAT STRANGE NIGHT bore witness to both the weakness and the strength of Inishnamona.

The blueprint for the action against Buckle left nothing to be desired, being as simple as it was brilliant. First, the gates he had so arrogantly slammed in the island face were to be blown up while he himself was at home. The noise would bring him running out to make investigations, at which a certain party was to slip inside Mount Skellin, leave a bomb with a burning fuse in a central position and then retire. The bomb was to explode before Buckle had time to get back, for there was no intention, at this point, of doing him bodily harm. The operation was purely a hint that his continuing presence thereabouts would not be welcome.

Everything promised to go off smoothly, as always when the people stood back to back. The charges had been laid in the dead of night, with no unauthorized person a penny the wiser, and on the day itself things seemed to augur well. The bomb setter patrolled the house in the morning, while Buckle was engrossed in the mulberry tree, to choose a site: it was the scent of his well-worn frieze that had bothered Snowdrop and Belle. There was the one slight check caused by the unforeseen arrival of Colonel Sentence with Sabina, but in barely half an hour they were homeward-bound again. No sooner had they gone than Bridie and Maggie, first collecting their geraniums and packing Mother Courage with the Infant of Prague in a basket, crept from the house in compliance with orders from the high command. As the hands of the clock moved on to zero hour, the prearranged signals, the owl-like hooting, were given and returned, and on the final note the button was pressed and the huge iron gates, with several trees and much of the grassy bank, rose high in the air and, in fragments, rained down upon the earth. And a few minutes later, just as everyone expected, Buckle came racing up to the scene of the crime.

But from that moment forth, nothing went according to plan. To begin with, Buckle was, inexplicably, not alone, and when the watchers finally grasped who his companion was, a chill of fear invaded every heart.

"O Lord, 'tis Mr. Boxham there!"

"O God, 'tis himself that's in it!"

"Didn't I say how he couldn't be dead, and he going off on the train?"

Such were the troubled murmurs that rose from the crowd. The feminine part of it stomped off in a body, with an air of having always predicted disaster.

Buckle made matters worse by looking neither angry nor

frightened; in fact, to the general mystification, he burst out laughing. "So someone has managed to shift the gates," he commented. "Good for him! It was quite beyond me."

Mr. Thomas was muttering a crack about "that well-known Irish specific, high explosive." But he was smiling too, even if grimly, and it wasn't every day of the week you would see the likes of that. It dawned on those present that once again their leaders had buggered everything up, and their terror mounted with every second as they awaited the explosion from the Big House yonder.

Not even the various side shows to which they were treated could divert their minds or reduce the tension. Major Floud drove up with his last gallon of gasoline, bringing Sabina, their arrival coinciding with that of the Colonel, on a bicycle, a sword across the handlebars and a bitch on either side. As the Major stepped out of his car, Snowdrop and Belle, excited as children at Christmas, seized and held him until they were whistled off, which, the Major declared, must have been done by the Colonel's wish and could only, as he put it, "cement the gulf which has risen between us." He retreated in dudgeon while Sabina walked over to Thomas and lashed him with her tongue, partly because the sight of him in the flesh reflated all her former animus and partly because he was here without her knowledge. Such doings, in the ordinary way, would have been a feast in themselves, but now they went almost entirely unheeded.

"God help us, Sab, don't make such a Judy of yourself!" her brother urged. Wheeling about, he strode up the avenue toward the house, dogged by the wrathful girl, with Buckle, still laughing, to bring up the rear.

Seeing them make for what might well be their deaths, the onlookers panicked. When Sergeant Foley cycled up in his turn, they eagerly buttonholed him, blurted out a part of the truth and begged him to intervene. What followed has ever since remained fraught with the ambiguity that attends on so much of Inishnamona life. Either the Sergeant was the bravest man in the world or he knew more about the bomb in question than the people chose to tell him.

For once again the local propensity to boundless ambition had triumphed over common sense. The blowing up of the gates, like that of the causeway, had been done with expert help from outside, but in the matter of the bomb the patriots had adopted a do-it-yourself policy, well-intentioned but unrealistic. The department gave generous grants toward the improving of fields, but on the condition that these were cleared of stones. Rather than dig out the heavy limestone boulders and cart them away, it was found pleasant and more convenient to blast them and bury the fragments nearby; upward of five acres at the monastery had undergone this treatment, to everyone's satisfaction. From preparing the charges required in it to the production of a full-scale bomb for domestic purposes had seemed to the euphoric local mind but a step; and contemplating the finished article, the patriots were proud indeed.

What went on in the Sergeant's head will never be known, but there is no disputing his actions. Heaving his bicycle over the ravaged ground, he leaped upon it and pedaled vigorously in the direction of the house, calling out to the trio as he passed that he would wait for them above and take their statements. On reaching the house, he walked straight in, fearless, located the bomb, saw that the fuse was out, picked up the whole contraption, hurried outside again and flung it over the parapet onto the shore, where it lies to this day, harmless as the pebbles all round it.

Relaxed, he lit a cigarette and strolled back to the house to wait for the others, and when they appeared, somewhat belatedly, Sabina and Thomas having frequently paused to bicker, he was there on the steps to greet them, friendly, sympathetic and radiating innocence.

The inquest, held in the library, was conducted throughout in the best and highest traditions of Inishnamona. No one knew anything; no one wished to complain; whiskey was produced and freely poured.

"And so it was to England you went, Mr. Thomas," the Sergeant said affably, once technicalities were out of the way. "And what did you think of that?"

"I only saw London," Thomas replied. "London's a fright."

"Didn't I tell you?" Sabina sneered.

"The boy writes home, Manchester is great," Sergeant Foley said, with a courteous inclination toward Buckle, as if he were somehow to thank for this. "If I had me time again, that's where I'd go."

"Dull old world if we all thought the same," responded Buckle. "Ireland forever! That's my motto."

They beamed at each other, and Buckle replenished the Sergeant's glass. Presently that officer took his leave and Buckle, aware that the Boxhams were spoiling to resume the fray, tactfully retired to bed. Brother and sister stormed at each other until both were spent, and then followed his example. Sabina went up to the room which had always been hers, and spent a long time glowering out of the window. The night had grown very still and heavy, and the first faraway rumblings of thunder began.

About a couple of hours later, Buckle awoke with the feeling that something untoward was going on. Through his window came flickers of light from the garden below, and there was a curious, bitter smell in the air. He jumped out of bed and ran to open the door, whereupon a cloud of smoke poured in, swirling about his head and driving him back. The house was on fire! Hurriedly he pulled on a dressing gown and rushed to alarm the others. Coughing and spluttering, the three of them made their way downstairs to the hall, where they soon ascertained that at present the fire was confined to the library.

"Foley's cigarettes!" Sabina exclaimed at once. "I saw him throwing the ends away, time after time, into the wastepaper basket!"

Thomas busied himself with the telephone, in a corner of the hall.

"No night service," Harry pointed out.

"I'll ring till she answers," Thomas snapped, suiting actions to the words, until Delia's sleepy voice came over the wire, asking what in the name of God was it now. She was much consoled by the news, however, and sounded positively cheerful as she undertook to inform those of the fire brigade who had a line, and to instruct them to alert the others.

Luckily, in the prevailing excitement, none of the crew had gone to bed, but various factors stood in the way of speedy service. The fire engine was lodged in a corner of the school playground at one end of the island, whereas Dermot, ferry master and tax collector, the only man who could drive it, lived at the other, and furthermore had been waiting for his telephone these seven years. Valuable time was lost in recruiting him, particularly as he had to be first persuaded the whole affair was not a cod. This difficulty overcome, and the crew at last assembled, the engine set off with a merry ringing of its bell, freely sprinkled by well-wishers with holy water against the impending storm, while Dermot strove to recall when gasoline last was put in the tank and how much, since the gauge had never worked.

They came safely to the bounds of Mount Skellin, however, and their next problem was that of access. The main approach being impassable, they had to enter by a side gate and run up a boreen which led to the stable haggart. The gate and posts, fortunately of wood, and worm-eaten as well, had to be demolished by ax before they could squeeze through the aperture, and when this was done, there was the uncertainty as to whether the shaky old bridge spanning the stream would bear the load. The crew helpfully jumped off to lighten it while Dermot with set face coaxed the vehicle over inch by inch, with the planks swaying and trembling beneath him. Once on the other side, the crew boarded again and they went their way with much improved morale, but all of a sudden the engine gave a little cough or two and died, the gasoline being exhausted. For the last two hundred yards of the way, the brigade had to push, slow work over the rough ground, made slower too since a large pile of timber had to be moved before they could enter the haggart.

"*Spät kommt Ihr, doch Ihr kommt!*" said Thomas sourly when at last they were there and ready to start work, for by now the fire was ranging freely over the lower parts of the house and licking its way up the stairs. Valuables still inside were left to take their chance now, those already rescued lay about in forlorn heaps on the grass.

"Don't confuse them, talking gibberish," Sabina rapped out. "It's great credit to them if they got here at all. They're not professionals, remember!"

There was small likelihood of anyone forgetting this point. It all-too-soon became clear that the crew had but the haziest notion of how to perform their task. No real fire had ever occurred in the district before; the nearest thing to one had been when the old Rector's chimney caught, after he burned a number of books whose content he could not approve. Twenty-five minutes ticked on before the hose was attached to the hydrant, and when this was finally done, there came the bitterest blow of all. Instead of the fierce jet of water they expected to play on the flames, as so often seen on television, after a series of croaks and gurgles there came only a thin, puling trickle such as would hardly extinguish a sod of turf. For this the summery weather was to blame and not themselves, but in Thomas' view it was a piece of deliberate, planned sabotage.

"Turn it on! Turn it *on!*" he kept howling at them.

"We have it so, right on to the full, Mr. Boxham, sir," was Pio's mournful reply. Among his many offices was that of chief fireman. "We'll never quinch the flames with the little drop of water that's in it!"

"What in God's name do I pay rates for?"

"Isn't that what all of us want to know? Would you like a word with Dermot?" For the people were apt to confuse the duty of collecting rates with that of providing value for them, and Dermot came in for many cruel words.

Thomas opened his mouth to blast him, but a deafening roar from the sky got in there first. The crew started as one and looked fearfully upward. Forked tongues of lightning streaked over-head, one after the other, illuminating the whole vast stretch of land and sea, followed by louder and louder bangs and reverbera-tions. Buckle turned to Sabina, thinking she might be in need of support and reassurance, but although the storm seemed to affect her powerfully, it was not in that kind of way. She was staring round her in fascination, now at the leaping flames, now at the angry sky, her eyes glittering with excitement, as if the disaster fulfilled some private longing of her own. Buckle was somewhat daunted by the look of her.

"You see? Neither of you will get it now!" she said, or rather crowed, with macabre triumph. "What a to-do about nothing it all has been!" She looked at him intently, hoping for signs of distress.

"What a strange girl you are," he murmured.

"Strange? Divil a bit of it."

"But your family house . . . that means so much—"

"—will all go up in smoke!" she burst in, savagely gleeful. "Everything here goes up in smoke sooner or later. It's the only ending possible."

"I don't think you are quite yourself," he said with a puzzled air. "Which is natural enough."

"What can you know about me? I've never felt more myself than at this moment." She resumed her contemplation of the storm and the burning house, rapt, isolated in pleasure, Buckle and the world forgotten.

And he thought to himself, Yes, what do I know of her, really, or of Thomas either, or of this whole land and its people?

Apparently solid figures here proved to be will-o'-the-wisps. The declared friend was the secret foe. What looked like perfect peace was in truth an endless, confused shindy about nothing of any importance. And in due course everything went up in smoke.

"Never in all my life have I seen such blithering incompetence," Thomas was fulminating.

"Ah now, Mr. Boxham! Sure, what can we do? Will we make a line to the sea and pass buckets? Will we do that for you?"

"There'll be forty yards between each man," said Thomas with the sudden calm of despair. "And we have no buckets," he added.

"Then what'll we do?"

"Whatever you like. I'm going to the lower stables, to bed," he called to the others. "There's hay down there, if we don't mind the rats. Are you with me?"

Buckle accepted the invitation; Sabina remained where she was, avidly watching. The skies broke and the rain teemed down on the scorching stone with hisses audible on the garden below, but still she stood there, drenched to the skin. The fire brigade consulted together and made off in a pack down the drive, coats over heads.

By morning the house was largely gutted, although the walls and the roofs had held. The ground was littered with glass from fallen windows. The sky was clear, the sun shone, the sea sparkled, the little waves broke softly on the shore. Water flowed steadily from the hose now that there was no occasion for it, the rainfall of the night having abruptly raised the catchment levels. Sabina lay curled up in the parapet, fast asleep, a look of tranquil contentment on her face. Thomas and Harry found her there when they emerged from their rustic bed.

"She's wet all through! She'll get a chill, pneumonia!" Harry protested in lively concern. "I quite thought she'd come in after us. But I was dog-tired and fell asleep at once. Look at her clothes, dripping water!"

"There won't be a feather off her, I promise," Thomas said, much surprised by his tone. "You sound as if you'd got rather fond of her! Now, there would be a fate worse than death." He looked down at the happy face and pensively rubbed his chin. "She's a deep one, though. I wonder, was it Foley's doing at all? Sabby was the last to leave the library."

"Don't, please don't!" cried Harry. "I really think there's enough in my mind that needs digesting, without any additions of that sort!"

The piteous note in his voice as he made the appeal caused Thomas to laugh outright. "All right, old chap, digest away," he soothed him. "And anyhow, we shall never know. Now I wonder, dare we venture in for a recce?"

Bravely they pushed the door and together entered the over-hot, smoldering husk of Mount Skellin. Sabina stirred, muttered something, smiled to herself and quietly went on sleeping.

About the Author

HONOR TRACY was born in Bury St. Edmunds, Suffolk, England. She received her preliminary education at a private boarding school in England; later she attended school in Dresden, Germany, and studied for two years at the Sorbonne in Paris.

From 1946 to 1953 Miss Tracy was a special correspondent in Europe and the Far East for the *Observer*, then Dublin correspondent to the BBC's Third Programme. At the same time she was associated with an Irish literary review edited by Sean O'Faolain, and also contributed short stories and articles to such American publications as *Vogue*, *Mademoiselle* and *Harper's Bazaar*.

Miss Tracy's first book was *Kakemono*, which dealt with the American occupation of Japan. Her second, a collection of essays entitled *Mind You, I've Said Nothing*, was published in 1953. Her reputation as one of the leading satirical humorists of the day was firmly established with her first novel, *The Straight and Narrow Path*, published in 1956. It was resoundingly praised by the critics, many of whom called it one of the funniest books of their experience. Miss Tracy returned briefly to nonfiction with *Silk Hats and No Breakfast* and *Spanish Leaves* (1964), and her novels published since *The Straight and Narrow Path* have been worthy successors: *The Prospects Are Pleasing* (1958); *A Number of Things* (1960); *A Season of Mists* (1961); *The First Day of Friday* (1963); *Men at Work* (1966); *Settled in Chambers* (1967); and *The Butterflies of the Province* (1970).